ALONE

After waiting for approximately five minutes, I opened the door to the pilot's compartment.

There was no one there.

The controls were steady as I watched them. The panel reflected the things that were happening. Altimeter, air speed, all the instruments were working nicely, but there was no one in that entire airplane except myself . . .

Here is a tale from the twilight zone of the weird and the terrible. A tale unlike any that you have ever read before. For only Charles Willeford could have created THE MACHINE IN WARD ELEVEN.

THE MACHINE IN
WARD ELEVEN

Also by Charles Willeford
and published by No Exit Press

Miami Blues

New Hope for the Dead

Sideswipe

The Way We Die Now

The Charles Willeford Omnibus:

(Pick-Up, The Burnt Orange Heresy and Cockfighter)

The Woman Chaser

Wild Wives/High Priest of California

The Machine in Ward Eleven

Charles Willeford

THE MACHINE IN WARD ELEVEN

FOUR WALLS EIGHT WINDOWS NO EXIT PRESS

Published in the United States by
Four Walls Eight Windows/No Exit Press
39 West 14th Street, Room 503
New York, N.Y.10011

www.4w8w.com

www.noexit.co.uk

October 2001

Copyright © Charles Willeford 1961

The right of Charles Willeford to be identified as author of this
work has been asserted by him in accordance with the Copyright,
Designs & Patents Act 1988.

All rights reserved. No part of this book may be reproduced, stored
in or introduced into a retrieval system, or transmitted, in any form
or by any means (electronic, mechanical, photocopying, recording or
otherwise) without the written permission of the publishers.

Any person who does any unauthorised act in relation to this
publication may be liable to criminal prosecution and civil claims
for damages.

ISBN 1-56858-210-2   The Machine in Ward Eleven

2 4 6 8 10 9 7 5 3 1

Printed and bound in Great Britain

Contents

Contents

Acknowledgments

Chapter I, *The Machine in Ward Eleven* was published by *Playboy* (1961) in slightly different form; Chapter II, *Selected Incidents*, appeared in *Gent* as *The Sin of Integrity*; Chapter IV, *The Alectryomancer*, appeared in *Alfred Hitchcock's Mystery Magazine*

THE MACHINE IN WARD ELEVEN

I LIKE RUBEN. He is a nice guy. He doesn't lock my door at night. He closes it, naturally, so that none of the doctors nor any of the other nurses will notice that it isn't locked when they're just walking past, but he doesn't lock it. (An unlocked door gives me a delicately delightful sense of insecurity.) And this is the kind of thing a man appreciates in a place like this.

A little thing here is a big thing; the differences between this place and the private hospital are much greater than fifty dollars a day.

Ruben also lights my cigarettes and, what's more, he doesn't mind lighting them. The day nurse, Fred, always appears to be exasperated when I call out to him for a light. I don't blame Fred, of course. The day nurse has many things to do compared to Ruben's duties. He has to get the hallway and latrines cleaned, the privileged patients off to O.T. And all of the meals are eaten during the day, too. Fred is responsible for the cart, the collection of the trays and spoons afterward, and so on. I've never had a chance to talk much to Fred, but at night, I talk to Ruben quite a little. Which means I listen, and that's what I need to do. There's a dark, liquid vacuum to fill. What Ruben tells me, I often remember. Like the cigarettes.

The American Red Cross furnishes each patient with a carton of cigarettes every week, although there isn't any limitation—at least I don't think there is—on how many cigarettes we can smoke in a week. A carton a week is plenty for me. But we aren't allowed to have matches or a lighter. The male nurse is supposed to open the cell door and light them for us when we call him. If the nurse is busy, a man has to wait, that's all. There have been times when I've had to wait so long that when Fred or one of the loose patients (there are quite a few of these loose ones who are allowed to carry matches, and they do little odd jobs around the hospital, only their work details are called "therapy.") came around to light my cigarette, I actually forgot what I called out for in the first place.

But at night it is different. The men in the other eleven (that number always makes my stomach feel queasy) cells in this locked ward are all good sleepers. Except for Old Man Reddington. Right after the supper meal, or within an hour or so, most of them are asleep. Old Man Reddington, in Number Four, has nightmares that are truly terrible. If I had nightmares like his I'd never go to sleep. But when I've mentioned his nightmares to him, he denied having any, so I guess he doesn't remember them. I wonder if I have nightmares? That's something I'll have to pump Ruben about some time. The reason I don't go to sleep early is because of my long, peaceful afternoon nap every day. I'm not allowed to go to Occupational Therapy, so when the other patients leave the ward for O.T. after lunch I'm locked in my cell. It's quiet then, and I sleep. I have nothing to think about; my memory is almost all gone, except for isolated, unsatisfactory, and unresolved little incidents. Trying to remember things, however, is a fascinating little game.

I like Ruben. He is a nice guy. Oh, yes, it was about the cigarettes!

"I don't really care, Ruben," I said to him the other night (I know it wasn't tonight), "but every week when the Gray Lady comes around with the cigarettes I get a different brand. And even though I'm satisfied with whatever brand I'm given, I don't think it's right. I realize that smoking is a privilege, but I've also concluded that any man who smoked all the time would sooner or later decide that he preferred one particular brand. And if he did, he'd buy and smoke the same brand all the time. Is it because we're crazy that we get a different brand every week, or what?"

Ruben frowned quizzically, and looked at me for a long time. He is a good-looking young guy (in a rather coarse way), twenty-five or six, with strong white teeth, and friendly enough, but when he examines me for a long time that way without replying I have a premonition that he doesn't truly like me, and that he might possibly be a doctor's spy. But then Ruben grinned fraternally, and I knew that he was all right.

"Do you know something, Blake," he said with unfeigned sincerity, "you're the only nut in my whole ward who's got good sense."

This incongruous remark struck both of us as funny, and we had to laugh. "No, seriously," Ruben went on, "that comment was a sign of progress, Blake. Do you possibly remember, from before maybe, smoking one particular brand of cigarettes? Think hard."

"No," although I didn't even try to think, "but this talk about cigarettes makes me want one. How about a light?"

"Sure." As he flipped his lighter he said, "If you ever do feel a preference for any particular brand, let me know. Nobody's trying to deliberately deprive anyone of their favorite cigarettes. But I've been working here for two years now, and you're the first patient who's ever mentioned the subject."

"Then maybe I'm not so crazy after all?" I smiled.

"Oh, you're crazy all right!" Ruben laughed. "Would you like some coffee? I'm going to make a fresh pot."

I remember this conversation well; the smoking of the cigarette; and yet I'm not absolutely certain whether he came back with the coffee later or whether I went to bed without it. I've had coffee with Ruben late at night on many, many occasions, but that particular night is a disconnected memory.

I cannot always orientate the sequence of daily events. It's probably because of the sameness here. The only real difference between day and night is that it's quieter at night (except for Old Man Reddington in Number Four); and there is quite a bit of activity in the mornings. Breakfast, the cleaning up, the doctor making his rounds, and I have my chess problems to puzzle over every morning. I work out two or three problems every morning, although I'd never admit it to Dr. Adams.

"A man's mind is a tricky thing, Blake," Dr. Adams said, the day he brought me the board and chessmen. He made this statement as though I were unaware of this basic tenet. "But if you exercise your brain every day— and I think you'll enjoy working out these chess problems—it'll be excellent therapy for you. In fact, your memory will probably come back to you in its entirety— all at once." He snapped his soft, pudgy fingers. "But I don't want you to sit around *trying* to remember things. That's too hard. Do you understand?" And he handed me an elementary paperback book of chess problems to go with the chess set.

"Yes, I understand, Dr. Adams." I nodded solemnly. "I understand that you're a condescending sonofabitch."

"Of course I am, Blake," he agreed easily, humoring me, "but solving chess problems is merely an exercise to help you. For instance, a person with weak arches can strengthen them by picking up marbles with his toes, and—"

"I haven't lost my marbles," I broke in angrily. "They've only rolled to one side."

"Of course, of course," he said wearily, looking away from me. I've learned how to discomfit these expressionless psychiatrists every time. I stare straight into their moronic, unblinking eyes. "But you will try to work some of the problems, won't you, Blake?"

"I might." A noncommittal answer is the only kind a headshrinker understands.

So I've never given Adams the satisfaction of knowing that I work three or four problems every morning. When he asks me how I'm getting along I tell him I'm still on the first problem in the book, although I've been through the book four times already—or is it five? Ah! Here's Ruben with my coffee.

The coffee is strong, just the way I like it, with plenty of sugar and armored cow. And Ruben is relating the story again about why he elected to become a male nurse. He's told me all this before, but each time he tells it a little differently. His fresh details don't fool me, however. He actually took the two-year junior college nursing course to be the only male student in a class of thirty-eight girls. But talking to me at night—or should I say, at me?—is probably good "therapy" for Ruben.

"By the way, Blake, your wife's scheduled to visit you tomorrow. You asked me to remind you."

"Already?" I made a clucking sound in my throat. "My, my, how time flies. It seems like only yesterday, and yet thirty happy, carefree days have sped by." I shook my head with mock dismay.

"Not for me," he said grimly. "Let me have your cup." And he closed my door.

I'm beginning to get accustomed to my wife now, but it was difficult at first. The first time she visited me I didn't even know the woman. I still don't recall marrying her or living with her before assuming the bachelor residence of this cell. But I had uncommonly good taste. Maria is a real beauty, still well under thirty, and she's a movie actress (she keeps reminding me). The first time they took me to the visiting room to see here I made the undiplomatic mistake of asking her what her name was —and she cried. I felt so sorry for her I've never made the same mistake again. Now, when I occasionally forget that her name is Maria I call her Honey or Sweetie-pants. She likes these pet names.

We usually spend our whole hour together talking about the movies, about technical details mostly, and she often asks me intelligent questions about acting techniques. (The doctor probably briefed her to ask me such questions to help me regain my memory, but I enjoy giving Maria advice.) I'm an expert in the field of falsely induced emotions, and although I don't remember directing any of the plays or movies or TV shows she told me I directed, I am apparently well-acquainted with all of the terms and practically every aspect of the craft—or so it seems. Maria may be lying to me, of course. It's quite possible that this vast store of film intelligence I dredge up and dispense with so freely during our monthly visits was gained by reading books on the subject before I came here. And it might be possible that a freak memory breakthrough allows me to remember film subjects as a person does who is blessed or cursed with a photographic memory. That isn't a bad *double entendre*: I think I'll mention it to Maria tomorrow—if I don't forget it by then.

But if Maria truly is an actress, she's a most convincing actress, because I always believe her when she tells me that I was a director. And there's a sharp, single scene that keeps recurring to me at odd and unexpected times, but it doesn't seem to be truly alive, despite the verisimilitude and living color. So whether it really happened, or whether it's an imagined scene I happened to create in my mind because Maria told me that I was a director—I simply do not know:

The sun is so hot!

This our fifth straight twelve-hour day on desert location, and this will be the twentieth episode of the series. Nineteen more to go after this one, and if Red Faris doesn't change his attitude soon, we'll never finish them all, which means, of course, that I will not. We may never finish this one, *The Pack Rats,* which is, in my skilled opinion, the lousiest script I've ever directed. But Red is brilliant; he knows *everything.* This is Red's third year as the star of the series, and he now owns a juicy fifty percent. A big, stupid, six-foot-two ex-football player who never had anything better than a walk-on at the Pasadena Playhouse before he lucked into this Western series, and yet he tries to tell *me* how to direct his scenes. And when I explain some basic acting rule to him he nods condescendingly, and winks broadly at the grinning crew members he plays poker with when he should be studying his lines.

Take Twelve coming up, far too many takes for the budget, but every time Red does some annoying little thing wrong. Purposely? I'm beginning to wonder. The scene is unimportant; even a poor take would be valid enough, but I seem to have some sort of uncontrollable compulsion to shoot it over and over again until it's perfect. The arid heat must be at least 110 degrees, but the enmity from everybody on the set is hotter than that, much hotter. They all hate me now, every one of them, they hate my guts. Wonderful!

"Okay, Red?" I grin pleasantly at our stupid star, who stands petulantly beside his sweaty gray horse. "I know I'm a real bastard, Red, but let's try it one more time. Rolling a cigarette is supposed to be a piece of business just as natural as breathing to a cowboy, and yet—"

"After riding across the desert, I'm supposed to be tired, Jake! And after about fifty goddamned takes—"

"Eleven," I emended cheerfully.

"—I'm not faking it! I *am* tired."

"All right, get mounted." I ignore his childish outburst, turn my back on him. "Here we go again, kiddies," I announce to the sullen crew.

No one moves; they avoid my eyes. They're looking past me toward Red Faris. I turn. Red is still standing stubbornly beside his horse. He glares at me, pouting with his upper lip only (which is no mean feat for a television actor). He looks toward the number one camera, raising his dimpled chin.

"That's it, everybody!" he shouts fiercely, in stentorian, but untrained pectoral tones.

A triumphant crew cheer mingles with the desert heat waves, thirty-one enthusiastic voices, including the script girl's parched, cigarette-contralto. My face freezes as Red winningly flashes his famous trademark, the sneer-snarlsmile, an endearing grimace which has been described with loving detail in seven trade mags.

"And on the way back," he calls out again, raising a long right arm (the football signal for free catch,) "the steaks are on me at Palm Springs!"

Another happy orgiastic rejoinder, followed immediately by the sounds of furious tearing down, leave-taking noises.

"I've been fired before, Red," I mention quietly, "but not this way, not crudely and publicly."

"Hell, you aren't fired, Jake! It's been a rough week, that's all. Danny (Danny Olmstead was the unit's chief film editor) can piece together at least one decent take out of the eleven, and if he can't," he shrugged, "we'll simply junk the scene. Okay, Jake?" Sneersnarlsmile. A patronizing hand reaches for my shoulder, but before it touches me I back away quickly.

"No, it isn't okay. I can't direct unless I have full authority. It's one of the little rules a good director lives by."

"Don't go hard-nosed on me; I haven't done anything to hurt your authority, J.C. I submitted damned well, I think, to every stupid idea you've had this week. And you know as well as I do, there isn't another star in television who'd go through eleven straight takes in a row without sounding off!" Sneersnarlsmile. "Look, Jake, we'll have us a few cold ones at the Springs, rustle up some girls and a few laughs—and Monday's another week. Right? There's no use getting sore—"

I swung for his dimpled chin—and missed. It should have been a fairly decent fight, but it wasn't. Although I'm shorter than Red, five-eleven, I'm well over two hundred pounds; but Red's hard right fist slammed into my jaw as if it contained a roll of nickels. And that's all I remember. The color film snapped. Clicketyclickety-clicketyclicketyclack, as the crazy reel rolled 'round and 'round the endless track.

At first, the thing-in-itself confused me. Bam! A slam in the jaw, no matter how hard, could not, or did not, at my initial awakening, add up to two thickly bandaged wrists. I was snugly warm, in bed; I was lethargically comfortable, and my wrists, bound with white gauze, didn't hurt at all. I was fighting the will to remember, and then total recall washed over the surface of my mind in a humiliating torrent:

No, I hadn't stopped with the gang in Palm Springs. I had driven my seagreen Porsche, top down, at a forbidden speed, all of the way home to my craggy redwood retreat in the Verdugo Woodlands above the L.A. smogbelt. A drink, alone on the sundeck, except for my fear. Economic fear. Failure fear. I had been wrong; Red Faris had been reasonable; I was through. Aware of this, I awaited the confirming telephone call. The sundeck was cool and breezy after a week in the desert. A dozen giant potted plants with green waxed leaves, placed strategically here and there, masked successfully the dusty chapparal of the steep olive-colored hills. In some kind of wild optimism my eyes returned repeatedly to the white telephone on the big circular coffee table. Would I finish one, two, three, or four drinks before it rang? The total was six, and I had just sat down again with number seven when—

"Jake-O, baby!" It was my agent, Weldon Murray.

"Willy, boy! Now don't tell me you've found a new

series for me already! You're the greatest, Willy—I shall not want—"

"I *did* manage to keep you on the payroll, Jake-O. Only you'll have to be satisfied with the standard director's contract—one-eighty per week. But it stays in effect until Red's series plays out—and that may be forever. I still haven't heard your side, baby, and everybody always has a side. If it's a fight they want, we can do that, too. Why didn't you call me first, baby? I didn't have any ammo to shoot with—"

"And I didn't have any to give you, Willy."

"I don't suppose, for just once in your life, that you'd be willing to cry a little, kiss and make up?"

"No, and it wouldn't do any good anyway. It's been coming on for weeks. And I'm tired, Willy, tired."

"I love you, sweetheart, but you're going to get a damned long rest this time, I'm afraid. Three is the fatal charm, it's been said in high places, and this is the third time for you in less than a year. They can't afford perfectionists in TV, baby—"

"I know."

"It's just that TV isn't the movies, and today even the movies can't—"

"Please. No lecture, Willy," I said wearily.

"Have you called Maria?"

"No. She's in London—I think."

"Want me to call her for you?"

"No, I'll call her later. But thanks, Willy."

After racking the phone I fished a squirming, many-legged arthropod out of my drink. How many men, I wondered curiously, are all washed-up at the age thirty-two meridional? Was I ahead of or behind schedule? And yet, I don't think that I was really depressed. I wasn't completely indifferent, but I had a rather sickening sense of relief. The useless struggle was finally over. The End.

I drank slowly, steadily, spacing my drinks, enjoying the silent evening and the yellow sky above Glendale far below. Hours, or many minutes later, I was giggling, lurching through the empty house in search of a razor blade. A sixty-thousand dollar home, mortgaged for seventy-five, a swimming pool, and no blades. How can a man slash his wrists with an electric razor? The phone kept ringing all the time. Needlers. Sympathizers. At last I found a blade, a used, rusty blade, in an old plaid train case that had belonged to my wife. The ancient blade had once nibbled persistent stubble from her long legs, in all probability. I giggled again as I eased the blade with concentrated caution into a fresh cake of soap. I didn't want to accidentally cut the fingers holding the blade—too painful—and yet I wanted to slice my wrists. Such paradoxical prudence was very amusing indeed.

The private hospital was a warm white womb.

There was a glass-enclosed porch parallel to the end of our ward, and the meals were served right on schedule in the dining room. I liked every one of my fellow eighteen patients—a charming, mixed-up group—and I would have been content to remain dormant in this friendly ward forever. My closest friend was Dave Tucker, an actor who had been possessed (literally) by the devil. He had played *The Devil and Daniel Webster* in summer stock a few months before, and while he was immersed in the role of Daniel, the devil had actually managed to get inside of his skin. Our unimaginative doctor, unfortunately, couldn't exorcise the devil from poor old Dave because the psychiatrist didn't believe that the devil was really under Dave's hide.

"The worst thing about Him, J.C.," Dave told me, scratching under his pajama jacket, "is the constant itching. He squirms around so much I itch all the time, and scratching can't get to Him."

Poor Dave. I believed him, of course. Why would any man lie about something like that? But I still couldn't resist giving Dave the business once in awhile. "Your case is the inevitable result of method acting," I told him, "but it could've been worse."

"How's that?"

"You could've been playing *Jumbo*."

"Move," he said irritably, clawing his chest, "it's your move." And we continued our chess game on the sunny porch.

I see now that it was a mistake to become friendly with Dave Tucker, or for that matter, with anyone. It hurt me too much—it was only a few days later—when the devil finally got him. We were playing chess again, smoking, not saying much of anything, when Dave urgently stage-whispered my name: "Jake! Get the doctor, somebody! He turned on the heat!"

I looked up from the chessboard, startled. Dave's handsome face was as fiery as a record jacket featuring exotic Hawaiian music. There was no perspiration; the devil had caught Dave in an unguarded moment, and he didn't even have enough time to perspire.

I rushed frantically into the ward, yelling my head off for the doctor. And I returned to the porch with Dr. Fellerman within a minute and a half—two minutes at most—but Dave was dead. The devil had boiled Dave's blood for him and fled. I was unreasonable then, more than a little hysterical, and I cursed Fellerman for all he was worth (which wasn't much), although it hadn't been entirely his fault. It.was a matter of time; the devil would have taken Dave sooner or later anyway. But the swiftness of the attack unnerved me, and I had a long, miserable crying spell.

After Dave, I dropped out of sight. No more friends for me. Not after Dave. I simply couldn't stand the emotional damage, and I was wise enough to see that much.

A truly successful, nigrescent depression has to be nourished, cherished. The strong rock wall can keep everything out and everything in, but it must be built stone by stone; each brick must be carved patiently from igneous rock; and every added layer must be layed meticulously, the stones so close together that no mortar is required.

Before retiring to my walled-in secret garden—before Dave—I'd been on the Camino Real, the road to recovery. All of the senseless oral and written psychological tests had been taken docilely; the tiny needles had been inserted into my scalp for the recording of the brain waves; and I had been a reluctant, but participating, member of Ward Fourteen's Group Therapy group. We met on Mondays, Wednesdays and Fridays at 11 A.M. in Ward Eleven, under the joint chairmanship of Doctors Fellerman and Mullinare.

There were four of us, not counting the two doctors (they merely observed and listened): Tommy Amato, a seventeen year old boy, the son of a well-known male movie star, and every night Tommy drowned his bed; Randolph Hicks, an ex-hotel manager who had deliberately crashed his car and now had a corrugated skull and a permanent eye-squinting headache; Marvin Morris, a pop songwriter, who, like me, had attempted suicide unsuccessfully—and there was me.

I never did understand fully what we were supposed to accomplish during these triweekly sessions. The doctors never uttered a sound; they sat impassively in their metal folding chairs looking us over like a pair of bespectacled owls caught out at high noon. We, the sick ones, were supposed to talk out our problems; I believe that was the general idea. But the atmosphere in the scaly, gray-walled ward was not conducive to talk of any kind; it was too depressing. The first five minutes of each meeting were always awkward, taut with the clearings of dry, apprehensive throats. Ward Eleven was an unused ward, pressed into service as a group therapy meeting place because of hospital space shortage, and we sat around in a rough semicircle, chain-smoking cigarettes. It was difficult to keep our eyes away from the six unoccupied mattresses—each covered with a soiled white sheet—on the floor near the doorway. The electro-shock machine rested on a small gray table in one corner of the room, and there was a padded, rubber-sheeted treatment table beside it. When the shock treatments were given early in the morning, the unconscious bodies were deposited on the mattresses until they awakened, and then the dazed patients were led away to eat breakfast. No, this ward was not an inspiring meeting hall to discuss problems of the mind.

It's against federal law to photograph nuts in a Funny Factory, but these group therapy sessions were great human comedies that should have been captured on film. They were the kind of comedies that cause streng men to weep copious tears. Albert McCleery would have loved to film them on television's old *Cameo Theater,* cutting back and forth from one face to the next.

After the nervous silence became almost unbearable, young Tommy was invariably first to break into the un-easiness.

"I wet my bed again last night." A simple statement of fact. Tommy was no longer embarrassed by his chronic enuresis, now that the doctors had convinced him that his was a psychosomatic condition, and he felt that we older men could help him. We were grateful to Tommy every time, of course, for breaking the sound barrier, and we wanted to help him.

"Ah, did you try elevating your feet?" Marvin would ask eagerly.

"Yes, I slept with three pillows under my feet last night, but they didn't do any good."

And then the group therapy session was underway. Once started, it was easier to talk than it was to just stare at each other. We discussed the movies, B.B., Russia, bridge, paperback novels, the quality of the hospital food, taxes, the L.A. traffic problem, the long distance dial system; everything; everything, in fact, except our individual and personal problems. Tommy, however, was always provided with fresh, thoughtful suggestions for *his* little problem—not that any of them ever worked. The two doctors never took notes, they never made any comments or suggestions, and they never attempted to steer our conversations. For their silence we were grateful, all of us, and I believe we did our best to entertain them so they wouldn't be too bored during their listening-in hour. But maybe the meetings did the doctors some good—I really don't know. After Dave, I refused flatly to attend the mental torture sessions anymore.

Ward Fourteen wasn't a locked ward, and within the hospital we had considerable freedom. There were movies at night (16 mm) in the patients' lounge. There was a library, a TV set on the porch, and there was a snack bar where the patients could sit around drinking coffee and eating sandwiches between meals. But I gave up these frivolous activities for the fulltime occupation of my uncomfortable bedside chair. I ate my three full meals every day, marching to the dining room with the others when it was our ward's turn to eat, but I returned immediately to my chair. After supper each night I went to bed, and slept dreamlessly until 6:30 A.M. I could've slept all the time, I think, but we weren't allowed on our beds during the day. Unable to drowse in my hard metal chair, I meditated and read, meditated and read again—and it was always the same book: *The Silent Life,* by Thomas Merton.

I was fascinated by these accounts of monastic life; the Carthusians, particularly, with their isolated hermitages, were brilliant men who had found the right answer to the complexities of life, and I was saddened by the knowledge that I could never be one of them. These holy monks had a curious mixture of humility and vanity I could never hope to achieve. They believed that if they were humble enough they would see God when they died —surely this was a naive vanity—so innocent and touching the tears welled from my eyes. But I knew that God would never look at a wretch like me. However, there was another path, and now that I had time to think—more time than I'd ever had in my life before—the tantalizing challenge appealed to me more and more. To reach the top wasn't really difficult; I'd been up there three times already—but the pyramid at the bottom was much broader.

How many American males had consciously directed every effort to achieving the absolute bottom of the pile, burrowing their way deliberately to the exact center of the bottom of humanity? If I could only get down there, really down, all the way down, without any outside help—ah!—here was a unique and terrible aspiration! How? How? An intelligent man could meditate for years on this fascinating challenge!

My deliberations were interrupted one morning by Dr. Fellerman. He had approached my bed in a surreptitious manner and tapped me on the shoulder. He asked me if I would like to talk to him alone in his office twice a week.

"I've got an hour open on Thursday, Mr. Blake, and another on Monday. I'll squeeze you in."

"Squeeze in somebody else," I told him coldly. "I have nothing to say to you." Unbidden, uninvited, he had interrupted a very important train of thought, and I glared at him to express my annoyance. Fellerman was a tall, almost cadaverous man, with a concave chest. His face was lined, tired; an ostensibly overworked man. In his loose, knee-length white coat, with his humped shoulders, and with his narrow head cocked to one side, he always reminded me of an unskilled mechanic listening to an unidentifiable engine knock.

"And you won't return to our little group therapy sessions, either?"

"No. But if I come up with a valid suggestion for Tommy Amato's bed-wetting problem," I said sarcastically, "I'll write it down and give it to him in the dining room."

I arose from my chair, turned my back on the doctor, and sat down again facing the wall, thereby terminating the unwelcome interview. This brief discussion took place on a Monday afternoon. On Wednesday morning, right after breakfast, the male nurse, Luchessi, told me that I had to visit Dr. Fellerman's office. Any mental patient has the privilege of arguing with his doctor, but only a crazy man will argue with a male nurse. Without protest, I accompanied Luchessi to Fellerman's private office.

"Mr. Blake," Fellerman said calmly, without preamble, "I've decided to give you a short series of nine electro-shock treatments." The sentence was a nail on a slate.

The hand, my right, carrying the cigarette to my mouth, was arrested in midair. I was frightened, yes, but my astonishment was even greater. The hair at the nape of my neck bristled; goose bumps crawled on my arms. The six, white-sheeted mattresses on the floor in Ward Eleven appeared vividly, sickeningly, in my mind. And the small electroshock machine, which resembled a cheap portable phonograph when the lid was closed, became a leather-covered symbol of terror—sudden, terrible death!

"No!" I blurted, shaking my head. "You aren't serious!"

He shrugged. "I don't know what else to do with you, Mr. Blake. You won't help yourself, you won't attend the group therapy sessions, you've refused private conferences. Do you still believe that it was the devil, instead of apoplexy, that killed your actor friend, Mr. Tucker?"

I said nothing; he was trying to trap me.

"You aren't getting any better, and the shock treatments will help you."

"Depression is something I can learn to live with," I said bitterly, "but I can't live with death."

"Now you're being melodramatic."

"Am I? How many people survive electric shock treatments?"

"The fatality percentage is so small it's practically unimportant."

"It's important to me! What is the percentage?"

"I don't know offhand; less than one fatality in every three or four thousand, if that high—"

"Nine treatments in a row drops those odds down to a damned dangerous level!"

"If we thought there was any real danger, Mr. Blake," he said quietly, "we wouldn't give you shock therapy. You're a strong healthy man, although you're a little overweight. To lessen the convulsion, we'll give you curare to relax you first."

"Poison? If the shock doesn't kill me, the curare will! Is that the idea?"

"I assure you, you have nothing to worry about. The treatments start tomorrow. Don't go to breakfast in the morning."

"And if I refuse?"

"Don't you want to get well?"

"Not if I have to take shock treatments I don't!"

"There's no pain, none whatsoever."

"I don't care about pain, but I don't want to lose my memory. My memories may be bitter, but they're all I've got left and I want every single one of them."

"There's a slight loss of memory, but it's only a temporary condition—"

"Well, I refuse to take the treatments. And that's final!" The cigarette burned my fingers, and I dropped it into his desk ashtray—a white ceramic skull. The ashtray alone, if more evidence was needed, gave the key to the psychiatrist's sadistic nature.

"The choice isn't yours to make," he reminded me gently.

"You're frightening me now, Doctor—"

"You needn't be. Your wife has consented to the treatments, and—"

"I don't believe you!"

"It's true, nevertheless. Don't build these simple treatments up out of all proportion in your mind. If all goes well, as expected, you may not need all nine of them. Sometimes six are plenty, and you'll be going home before you know it."

"But I don't *want* to go home," I wailed unhappily. The tears I could no longer restrain washed my face. "All I want, all I ever wanted, is to be let alone . . ." Blubbering childishly into my sleeve I stumbled blindly out of the office and Luchessi took me back to the ward.

Later, and considerably calmer, I realized upon reflection that most of my knowledge about electroshock therapy had been learned second-hand from a fellow patient, Nathan Wanless, during idle bull sessions on the porch. Unintentionally, Nate had implanted dread of the little machine in my head by innocently underplaying the description of his own course of treatments.

"I didn't mind too much, Mr. Blake," he told me quietly. His eyes already had a puzzled expression, and at the time he had only had three treatments. "On the first one I asked to go first, you see, because I was a little scared and wanted to get it over with. I climbed up on the table in Ward Eleven and four male nurses—Luchessi's one of them—grabbed me by the pajamas and bathrobe. One guy held both feet. When the old electricity shoots through your brain you get one hellova big convulsion, and if these guys didn't hold you in a tight brace you'd get your back broken. It'd snap like a match. Anyway, Dr. Fellerman slipped the little harness over my head, and it's got a chromium electrode that clamps tight over each temple. Then they stick a curved piece of rubber hose in your mouth to bite down on and that's it."

"What do you mean, that's it?" I asked him tensely.

"Blooey, that's all."

"Blooey?"

"Blooey. I didn't feel anything. Next thing I know I'm awake and looking up at the ceiling, flat on my back on one of the mattresses in Ward Eleven. You know the—"

"I know, I know. But what did you feel? Did you have any screwy dreams while you were out, anything like that?"

"No, just blooey, that's all. One minute I was wide awake, a little scared, looking up at Dr. Fellerman, and then I was on the mattress looking at the ceiling instead. A funny feeling. Soon's the nurse sees you're awake, he sends you across the hall to the little kitchen in Ward Ten for scrambled eggs. Ward Ten's the locked ward, you know."

"I know. But there must be more to the treatments than that, Nate. You make the whole business sound too simple."

"It is simple, Mr. Blake. The second time I watched some of the other guys take theirs to see how it worked, and that was it. Soon's the electrodes are in place Dr. Fellerman turns on the two knobs on the machine. There can't be more'n one hundred and ten volts, because the cord's just plugged into the wall socket. All the same, I imagine Dr. Fellerman watches the needle pretty close."

"What needle?"

"There's a needle on the gauge. The machine might be pre-set, but I don't think there's any rheostat, so when the needle hits the right number on the gauge the doctor turns off the machine. And that's it."

"The patient on the table. What kind of a convulsion does he have?"

"You can't really tell, not with all those guys holding him and all. All in all, I guess it's a very humane machine. I imagine the electric chair works the same way when they execute somebody. They put the guy in the chair, flip the old switch, and blooey, that's all. Of course," Nate frowned thoughtfully, "they have to strap the guy into the electric chair because the electricity's so much more powerful." He giggled. "The guy's back must get broken anyway, but he's dead by that time so it doesn't make any difference."

"The analogy—electric chair and shock machine—doesn't seem humane to me, Nate." I shuddered.

"Why not? It doesn't hurt you none. Blooey, that's all, except that on shock treatments you wake up later. In the electric chair you don't—not in this lousy world anyway."

Nate Wanless was no longer with us. The course of shock treatments had helped him—perhaps they had eliminated his mental depression altogether—and he had been discharged from the hospital. But after a few treatments he'd developed a frowning, perplexed expression. He was unable to recall entering the hospital, or any of the events that had led up to his admission. I had talked to him several times before his release, and except for his memory block, which worried him very little, he was a rational, perfectly normal—nothing—that was it, nothing! He was neither excited nor depressed. He was stonily indifferent to his past and future, and he had *believed* Dr. Fellerman when he was told that his memory would return, all in good time.

But I didn't believe it, not for a damned second I didn't!

My palms were wet. My throat was dry. For the first time in my life I knew true fear! Ordinary fear was a familiar emotion I'd known intimately, many times—the fear of losing an arm or a leg or an eye in battle, when I had fought (for a blissfully short three months toward the very end) in Korea; the fear of being absolutely broke; the fear of success and the fear of failure; and certainly, the fear of death. And I had also known that secret, unvoiced fear, the kind no one ever admits to anyone, and only rarely to himself; the unknown terror of afterdeath. Is there an afterlife or is there not? And if there is, how will a man fare there? Will he be able to withstand the punishment meted out to him according to his earthly record?

But what were any of these childish, mundane fears in comparison with the worst fear on earth, the worst possible misfortune that could happen to mortal man? The fear of becoming a vegetable. Could any misfortune be worse?

His memories, his ability to laugh at his follies and stupidities—when the chips were finally down, these were the only things a man had left to him. Otherwise, a man is a pine tree, a turnip, a daisy, a weed, existing through the grace of the sun and photosynthesis during the day, and ridding himself of excess carbon dioxide during the long night. I was still a fairly young man; if the choice had been the simple one of life and death I could have accepted it, I believe, at any age. Perhaps I could have even feigned some kind of insouciant bravery if I had to choose death—I didn't really know.

But I had only to go to the glass windows on the porch and look out over the verdant hospital grounds. From the windows I could always see three or four hospitalized human vegetables sitting on their benches beneath the sun. Most of them were old men, white-thatched, harmless, of course, and when the weather was nice they were allowed to remain outside all day long. They never bothered anyone, they didn't think, they couldn't remember anything, not even their names, and their ability to laugh was completely gone. Plants. Vegetables.

Mental patients live for an uncommonly long time, and I was only thirty-two. I was also gifted with that accursed trait that every director or actor must have to achieve any measure of success in the world of make-believe: the ability to put myself into someone else's place. Empathy. I could project myself now into the future, near and far; Blake the Vegetable, sitting in the sunlight year after year until he was a feeble, drooling old man of eighty—no, ninety!—the damned busy-body medicos were learning more about geriatrics every day.

No longer was I J.C. Blake the Arrogant, the one man in Hollywood who had never taken anything from anybody. I was transformed instantaneously by my cool, logical imagination into Blake the Abject, Blake the Beggar, Blake the Craven. All right, then. If Dr. Feller-man wanted me to crawl I would crawl. If he wanted me humbled, if he wanted his feet washed, I would wash his feet and anoint them with scented oils. The gelid dread that twisted my entrails was panicky, and there was so little time! The clock above Luchessi's desk told me that it was 11:40. I had to see Fellerman now, before he left the hospital at noon. When tomorrow morning came it would be too late; they would inject their South American curare into my veins and then destroy my fine mind forever with their machine. Controlling my inner conflict as well as I could I approached Luchessi's desk.

"You should've reminded me," I said, smiling, "about the group therapy session in Ward Eleven."

"I thought you dropped out of group therapy?" But he wasn't suspicious; he was already filling in a hall pass for me.

"I did, Luchessi, but I was supposed to start back today. That's what the doctor wanted to see me about this morning."

"You're late, you know." Luchessi frowned as he handed me the pass. "But it isn't my fault."

"I know; it's mine, but I simply forgot about it. It's probably too late to go at all now, but if I didn't make the attempt Dr. Fellerman would say that I was being uncooperative. You know how he is."

"Sure. You'd better get a move on."

I had escaped legally from the ward, and if an official stopped me in the corridor on my way to Ward Eleven the pass would be a valid ticket. When I reached the ward the group therapy meeting was just breaking up. Tommy

Amato was the first patient through the door. I nodded absently to him before he could start a conversation, brushed by the other three emerging patients and entered the ward. Dr. Fellerman and Dr. Mullinare were still seated in their metal chairs at the far end of the ward— holding a post-mortem on the session, I supposed. I hesitated, not allowing myself to look to the right, toward the shock machine and treatment table.

"Well, hello there, Blake!" Mullinare called out cheerily. "Long time no see." (This Mullinare character was a real cornball.)

"Good morning, Dr. Mullinare," I responded plëasantly. "Sorry to intrude on you gentlemen this way, but I wanted to talk for a few moments with Dr. Fellerman." I moved toward them, holding myself erect, my back stiff.

"That's quite all right, Blake," Fellerman said. "We're finished here." He winked at Mullinare. "Call me tonight, Kevin, and we'll see."

"Sure." Mullinare clasped my shoulder with a meaty, sweaty hand. "We've missed you at our little sessions, Blake," he said lightly.

"I've missed them, too, Doctor," I lied. "Perhaps Dr. Fellerman will let me rejoin the group."

Mullinare didn't reply. He left the ward, closing the doors behind him. I wet my parched lips, wondering how to begin. The rehearsed, practiced silence peculiar to psychiatrists puts every patient on the defensive from the first moment on. These doctors rarely, if ever, ask questions, except perhaps with their incurious, unblinking eyes. But even their eyes are distorted unnaturally, as a rule, behind glasses. Fellerman, his skinny shoulders hunched, his narrow head cocked to the right as he looked up at me from his seated position, gave me no help. How could any man, a human being, approach such a machine?

"I've been hoping, sir," I began humbly—and I regretted the lack of a Balkan peasant cap that could have been snatched respectfully from my head as I began to address him—"that you might reconsider your idea of putting me on shock treatments. My attitude has been poor all along, sir, and I realize that now. And I apologize, most sincerely. If I am to help myself, I must cooperate fully with you and the other doctors. And I want you to know, Dr. Fellerman, I'm ready to turn over a new leaf. If you'll only allow me to do so, I'll return gladly to the group therapy sessions. And if you still have those two free hours open you mentioned I'd like to take advantage of them, too. Why," I smiled, "when I finally got it through this thick dumb head of mine, Doctor, that I was only hurting myself by my incorrigible attitude, I began to feel better right away. Yes, sir, and that's the truth! Why I'm not nearly so depressed as I was when I talked to you earlier this morning!"

I essayed a light laugh then, and it was indeed a pitiful, strangling sound. Is there anything more heart-rending than the forced sound of false gaiety?

"And what's more, sir," I plodded on, "I think my change in attitude will be beneficial to my fellow patients, too. I really do. Outside in the hall just now, when I bumped into Tommy Amato, my heart went out to that young boy. I realized how selfish I've been all along, thinking only of myself instead of others. And as you remember, Doctor, I talked quite a bit at group therapy, just as much if not more than any of the other patients. I've got a *good* mind, Dr. Fellerman, and if I truly put all of my intelligence to work, I'll bet you any amount you care to wager that I can come up with a valid solution to Tommy's bed-wetting problem. Yes, sir! If you'll just cancel those shock treatments I'll get a notebook and pencil and I'll start working on young Tommy's problem right away. I know it sounds funny, now that I'm a mental patient, but when I was in college I got straight A's in Logic. And I'll just bet you, sir," (for a brief instant I considered injecting another forced, merry little laugh into my monologue, but I swiftly changed my mind, knowing I couldn't pull it off convincingly) "that once I solve Tommy's problem I'll also solve my own!

"From what little knowledge I have about Freud—of course, I don't pretend to know nearly as much as you do, what with your wonderful training and the brilliant record you've established, and. all—but it's a sign of progress, isn't it? I mean, when a mental patient begins to think about the feelings of others instead of just himself, isn't that a sign of recovery? Well, maybe not. But what I want to get over to you is that I'm not in any badly depressed state any longer. Shock treatments are for people who really need them, and when we get into our private consultations—just the two of us—I don't like to confess too really personal experiences in a group therapy session, but when it's just you and me, I'll tell you everything!"

I lowered my voice confidentially, to an intimate level. "Sex, for instance. I know how interested you psychiatrists are in sex, and you are aware, of course, that I'm married to Maria Chavez, the movie star. Well, when we were first married we were very much in love, you see. And we did all kinds of things together when we made love. I know you're anxious to go to lunch now, but when we meet alone I'll tell you every tiny detail. I'll make some notes, so I don't forget a single moment of it. With my screen experience I've learned how to tell a story well, and I'll tell you all about our love life together so you'll be able to get a real vicarious thrill out of it. I'll do anything, anything, only please, please, please—!"

I was unable to continue; my invention had flagged. Dr. Fellerman's expression hadn't changed once. Nothing I had said (or possibly could say) made any impression on the man. I dropped abjectly to my knees and kissed his shoes. He wore black, rather old-fashioned, high-topped shoes, and white socks. I was furious with myself because I couldn't cry. The needed tears refused to flow, and I had a desperate need for every crutch on the emotional scale to elicit sympathy from this stone, this dehumanized machine.

"Get up, Blake, get up from the floor," Fellerman ordered quietly.

"Yes, sir." I scrambled hurriedly to my feet. "You'll take me back into group therapy, sir? And you won't put me on shock treatments?"

He got up, stretching his long skinny arms as he yawned, and *yawn* he did. "No, Blake, I'm convinced that electroshock treatments will do you a lot of good." Without a backward glance he started toward the exit doors.

Before he took three steps I caught up with him. My fingers dug into his neck before he could cry out. He struggled, but he didn't have a chance. I kicked his feet out from under him and followed him to the floor, still clutching his scrawny neck. I squeezed relentlessly until my fingers tingled with pain, but the moment I was positive his limpness was unfeigned I dragged his unconscious body to the treatment table in the corner. Using ripped strips of a sheet I took from one of the mattresses on the floor, I quickly tied his body to the table. As I began to stuff his slack mouth with wadded paper towels from the pile on the smaller table, Fellerman gagged slightly and opened his eyes. Without his thick glasses, which had been dislodged during our unrehearsed wrestling match, Dr. Fellerman's big brown eyes were very expressive indeed, particularly when my fumbling fingers adjusted the elastic harness over his head and I centered the shiny electrodes to his temples.

A simple, impersonal, uncomplicated machine. I plugged the long cord into the wall outlet, turned the two plastic knobs as far to the right as they would go and left them there. The sensitive needle on the gauge banged against the red plus-pole so hard it almost bent, jiggled slightly, and remained there without a quiver. The body convulsions were terrible to see, and I turned my head away. I couldn't bear the sight of this long, skinny body buckling and jerking beneath the steady flow of electricity. I lit a cigarette and left the ward. As I hurried down the corridor (it was time to get into the lunch line for the march to the dining room) I considered the involved technical problems of capturing this unusual scene on film. Handled exactly right, the scene would scare the hell out of any average movie audience. Good background music was mandatory. When a man takes six or seven aspirin tablets his ears ring; this amplified ringing sound would be excellent on the sound track. But if the scene weren't done perfectly—only one little slipup, and a nervous audience would burst into a giggling, embarrassed type of laughter. A point of view would have to be decided upon—Fellerman's or mine? Here was a scene that couldn't be left to the discreet, unblinking eye of the camera—no.

My transfer to the state hospital came through quickly, but I was never given electroshock treatments. They gave me insulin shock treatments instead. Every morning they awakened me at 3 A.M., dragging me down the corridor kicking and screaming to a dark little room where I was tied hands and feet to another bed and my veins were filled with insulin. And there they destroyed my mind—or so they thought. The dreams under insulin were too real to be dreams, but I finally had enough of the horrors to stop fighting them. And when I stopped fighting them, they stopped the treatments. My spirit isn't broken yet, but they don't know it, by God!

"_____!"

"Are you all right, Blake?" Ruben's voice is genuinely concerned. "What's the matter?"

"I'm all right, Ruben. Every once in a long while a peal of that screwy laughter gets away from me inadvertently. I'm sorry. But after all, if I weren't crazy

I wouldn't be locked up permanently in the State Asylum for the Criminally Insane—or would I?"

"Take it easy, Blake. You don't want to get Old Man Reddington started, do you?" He closed the door; this time he locked it.

I like Ruben. He is a nice guy. But I'll have to watch myself more carefully, particularly that wild dramatic laughter. So long as I keep my big mouth shut and do everything they tell me to do (within reason), I'll be able to stay here forever. I doubt if they would ever try me now for the murder of Fellerman, but if they found out that most of my memory has returned, they'd return me to the outside world again as soon as they could. After all, I still haven't reached rock bottom yet, and I must bear in mind that the competition for my hard-won private cell is getting keener all the time.

All the time. . . .

SELECTED INCIDENTS

The only art and the only creation possible to humanity is that of giving new form to an old idea.

Anatole France

WELL—you're right on time, Charlie. Come in, come in! Sit down. Drink?

I'll pour one for you, anyway, whether you drink it or not. It's a sort of stupid rule I have—at least here in the office. I happen to want a drink, and I don't feel right when I drink alone. One won't hurt you; *one* drink never did anything to anybody.

To tell you the truth, I—that's funny, isn't it? To tell you the truth. Christ; that's what I've been doing for an hour every day since you started to write my autobiography. Telling you the truth. How long has it been now?

That long, eh? Well, there's no big hurry about the book. And the first three chapters you finished were first rate, Charlie, absolutely first rate. As I told you before, my wife was after me for months to write my autobiography, but I hesitated, kept putting it off. A lot of these "as told to" autobiographies sound so damned much alike; the way they read, I mean. Especially our Hollywood variety—the entire industry's less than sixty-five years old. And if you read many of the biogs you start running into the same stale anecdotes and stories, except that they're attributed to different people in different books. You keep that in mind, Carlos; I don't want my

36

autobiography to read like any of these tired stereotypes—

No, it reads fine, at least the first three chapters. But you know what I mean. Names'll be dropped, naturally, but I still want the book to be my personal story. One of the reasons I put off starting it so long was on account of the new trend. When Groucho Marx wrote his autobiography all by himself, a lot of us out here didn't like the idea at all. It was damned presumptuous of him, if you ask me. The trend was started, however, and although most of the stars and old-time producers still have their books ghosted, they now feel that they have to say that they were written on their lonesome. Groucho didn't have his book ghosted; I know that as a fact.

But the more I thought about the idea, especially after I tried to make some preliminary notes and so on, the more disgusted I got. After all, I pay writers to write scripts, studio publicity, ads, my letters, and everything else for God's sake, so why should I try to write my own autobiography?

I'm a producer, not a writer, and if a man wants a professional writing job he hires a professional writer. Besides, with your name on the "as told to," the books'll sell better. You've established a reputation in this field, and your name on the cover along with mine lets the book buyers know that it's a professional job.

Have it your way, Chaz. But the book'll sell well regardless, even if Cheetah was the co-author. Remember, I've got ten different series working these days on the networks. And that fact means all the network book plugs I want, ingenious plugs, too. You can sell anything on TV, Charles, and that's a fact. It's a matter of percentages, and with enough plugs my autobiography would be a best seller if you wrote it in Sanskrit. I've never tried this, but I know it would work—if I were to advertise on TV that viewers could have their right arm cut off, absolutely free, simply by reporting to such-and-such a hospital by 10 A.M., a certain percentage of tele-viewers would show up at the hospital the next morning with their right sleeves rolled up.

It isn't funny, Chaz, it's a matter of percentage ad-vertising and good copy. So any man who writes his own autobiography when he isn't a professional writer is simply feeding a big fat ego . . . And that goes for all these weird generals, too, not only movie personalities.

I'm having another drink—how about you?

Suit yourself. No—don't hook up your tape recorder, and no notes today, either. As I started to tell you when you first came in—I intended to call you at home and ask you not to come at all today. I'm rather upset this morning. That mess—perhaps you read it in the *Times* this morning?

J.C. Blake, slashing his wrists. A terrible thing. Of course I knew Jake; I knew him well. According to the publicity, I was the producer who first discovered him. I didn't, of course, although I may have helped him up the ladder for a few rungs, at least in the beginning. But that doesn't mean anything. If I hadn't helped him, some-one would have had to—a damned talented director. But more than talent, he had conviction of purpose and drive. Talent by itself means nothing, as you know yourself, Charlie. But as I say, this hour was already kept open for you, and if I'd canceled our appointment, I'd have been sitting in here brooding about J.C. Blake. So, well, you're here, and for the dough I'm paying you, you can afford to waste an hour.

No, not at all. I don't mind talking about J.C. I just don't feel like talking about myself, that's all; telling you how great I am and everything when a director like Blake is in the hospital—maybe the morgue by now—with two slashed wrists.

Incidentally, did you ever see the wreathes I send to funerals? I have them made up special by the Norton Floral Company—they're beautiful things. Round, in the shape of a film can, you see, with my message in two words in tiny red rosebuds: "We Remember." Then the name, of course. "Elgee Productions." If there's anything I hate, it's these cheap people who put notices in the paper—"Don't send flowers." To send flowers is a beautiful gesture; it shows that we have respect for our dead out here, that's all. And if you've ever attended one of these funerals where they didn't have any flowers, you'd know what I mean.

Blake? You never met him? It's just as well. Nobody ever really knew him anyway—not really. Perhaps it's the difference between a biographer like you and a novelist. I can talk to you easily, but I can't talk to a novelist for five minutes. They don't listen, you see—they're thinking of something else all the time. Blake was that way; he was a film maker, but he was an artist, you see.

The first time I met J.C. I thought somebody was pulling a practical joke on me—it was really funny— but it worked. He had a gimmick; even a man as talented as J.C. Blake had to have a trick to put himself over. It's almost a rule out here—the way a man has to keep topping himself and others to get ahead.

Yes. He had an appointment all right. Certainly. But it was only for ten minutes. And yet he stretched it out for more than an hour, and went to lunch with me besides.

What? You're damned right I haven't taken you to lunch yet. And I don't intend to! I don't eat lunch anymore; I eat cottage cheese, and sometimes a cup of hot bouillon. And I eat alone. I simply can't stand to see some healthy irresponsible writer like you eating steak and french fries when I'm forced to eat cottage cheese. Anyway—yes—to get back to Blake.

He had an agent, and his agent made the appointment for him. That's another rule. If a man doesn't have an agent he's a nonprofessional and I don't talk to him. I can't even see all the professionals I should see, let alone amateurs.

I was also vaguely aware of Blake's name. In this business, you have to keep up with those people who've got something on the ball. And the reports, in synopsis form, come in all the time.

Blake had already directed a play in New York, and it had received above average critical acclaim. It was one of those weird, sadistic off-Broadway things. Most of these crazy New York plays are awful things nowadays —incest, cannibalism, homosexuality, insanity, every taboo forbidden to us on TV—and they pass back there as entertainment. It's the current trend. A good many of these plays are written by screenwriters, because— as they put it, "television censorship stifles their creativity." Which is all a lot of crap, because we buy the same sick plays that hit it on Broadway, clean them up, add entertainment values, and make them into fairly decent movies.

And nine times out of ten, Chazz, the same guy who wrote the play also gets a nice fat fee to write the movie adaptation and to make the mandatory revisions. So where is his so-called artistic integrity then? It's just another gimmick, that's all. The same tourists who visit New York on a vacation, and sit drooling through some of these sadistic plays—paying scalpers ten bucks a ducat—would flood us with indignant letters if we gave them the same plays for absolutely nothing on televsion.

In any event, Blake had directed this one play, and it had considerable notoriety value, despite a short run, but it wasn't made into a movie. It was one of those anti-dramas, as I recall—no story, just mean and meaningless dialogue by several mean characters. The studio that bought the play got stuck with it. They could've fixed up a story all right, but the title was too long for a theater marquee. Without being able to use the original title, getting the benefit of the publicity value, there was no use fooling with the play. Exhibitors don't like long titles for their marquees.

But Blake was more than just a sometime legitimate stage director. He'd made a couple of avant garde sixteen millimeter films, and although I hadn't seen either one of them at the time, I had heard about them. The motion picture is an art form, Charles, all of us know that, and most of us keep private film libraries at home the way book publishers keep home libraries full of books. A man doesn't reach my position in the industry without a knowledge of art. That's something you might remember for my autobiography. Later on, I'll show you my film library, run off a few unusual films for you. It may open your eyes as to what we could really do with movies if the public would let us make a little money out of them in the bargain.

The point is: we keep abreast of the avant garde trend in the sixteen millimeter film club circles and rentals. The improved sixteen millimeter equipment, and the cheaper sound processing techniques, have brought a lot of gifted amateurs into film-making for the various film societies. Sometimes we pick up one of these devoted cinematographers who has a knack for special effects and give him a job in the technical department.

When Blake was ushered into my office, however, his personal appearance was definitely against him. He had a short red beard and a thick moustache. His hair was coal black, and too damned long. A lot of dark-haired men sprout red beards, but a beard of any color is held against a man out here. Every fall semester I conduct a seminar at U.C.L.A. for graduate students who are working for their master's degrees in Cinema, and I always stress to these young men that they should observe conservatism in their dress and personal appearances. Cinema, whether it's television or movies, is a business. We must present a concerted public image, and there's no place in any business for nonconformists and eccentrics.

But I was distracted from Blake's appearance by all of the equipment he had with him. He had a sixteen millimeter projector, a portable screen, and a can of film. The moment he came in he started to set all this stuff up, right here in the office, without saying a word.

"Look, Blake," I said to him, "your appointment's only for ten minutes."

"Make it twelve," he replied, "I've got a film to show you."

I had to smile. We've got a dozen comfortable projection rooms here at the studio, and here's a man setting up a projector and screen in my office for a home movie arrangement. I mentioned this to Blake, and he said that he was aware of my various studio projection rooms.

"My films are designed for small groups," he said, "from three to ten people at most, and they should be shown in small intimate rooms—not in theaters. So I want you to see the film under normal conditions."

This wasn't an original idea, of course. We always try to keep in mind that our television plays are to be seen by small groups and families, but it was a different idea for a movie to be planned this way. Interested by the idea, I allowed him to go ahead with the preparations, and I even lowered the venetian blinds myself.

And now, Charles, I'm going to speak pontifically—a bad habit I've picked up from these lecture and seminar sessions at U.C.L.A.—but ours is a private conversation; so I can let myself go a little bit with you. With colleagues, this is a side of myself that's best to keep submerged.

But Blake flattered me, and I responded to this type of flattery. He didn't insult my intelligence by going into an involved explanation, the way I'm doing with you because I don't have the film to show you. He merely showed the film. Within a few dozen frames I recognized where he got his inspiration, and what he was trying to do. When it comes to art, there's nothing really new, you know, not if you've thoroughly explored the subject.

Back in the tenth century, in China, most of the artists were subsidized by the court, or they managed to get commissions from the wealthy. These were the professionals. But there were quite a few gifted amateurs with private means who also painted, and these people began to break with traditional forms. A parallel today is the new interest by private individuals who are making their noncommercial sixteen millimeter films.

The Chinese amateur painters weren't faced with deadlines; they had plenty of time at their disposal and they used it, you see. You may not be aware of it, Chaz, but the entire movie industry is based upon a biological accident—the fact that the retina can retain an image for a momentary period. When the next frame appears, the remembered frame is retained long enough to merge with the next one, and we then have the appearance of movement. Movies don't slither through the projector; each frame stops for a moment—held in place by the maltese cross before the next frame appears.

I'm sorry, Charles. I know this is basic knowledge today, but not too many people realize that many of the finest painters in China during the late tenth century were also aware of the same phenomenon.

But Blake knew it, and somehow, he must've known that I did, too. The Chinese painters—this was during the latter period of the Five Dynasties—painted landscapes on scrolls, some of them more than fifty in length. One person, two or three at most, would sit down and unroll the scroll from right to left, and only a small section of the painting could be seen at a time. The sequence of the scroll required a good memory—moods, motifs and details were often repeated, and they had to be remembered for a full appreciation. The perspectives also were shifted—but to return to Blake's film, which was what we call pure cinema, he'd accomplished the same thing.

Only by using moving images, it sure as hell taxed your memory and your skill as a movie-goer. The title was *Selected Incidents;* storyless, plotless, of course, but it was a beautiful showcase for Blake's talents and to show his mastery of the medium. There were a series of tight shots; the overall impression of the montage gave an impressionistic viewpoint of a drunk's outlook on the world —a drunk or a schizophrenic's—but that isn't important in pure cinema. The viewer has to work when he sees a film of this kind and, depending upon his own knowledge, experience, and personal contributions to his seeing, well, every viewer can very easily have a different interpretation.

There was no sound, no subtitles; merely images merging skillfully, evenly, and flowing like a fast mountain stream. A closeup, for example, of a thickly coated dark tongue—and almost before you recognized it for what it was, the image was followed by a black, wet asphalt street, which led, in turn, to a black velvet coat collar, and so on.

A short, but very impressive film. And I recognized something else. A layman, Carlos, probably wouldn't recognize it, and it isn't easy to describe precisely what I mean. How Blake managed the thing so early in his career, I don't know, but he had developed a personal cinematic style.

Take a look, for a moment, at that unhappy clown on the wall above the couch. It's a Roualt, as you know, twenty-five thousand bucks worth of oil paint. Incidentally, I didn't buy the painting as a hedge against inflation; I bought it because I like it.

Everyone knows that Roualt had a distinctive style; you can recognize an original Roualt as far as you can see one. His style is inimitable. Most painters—you might say all of them—have a distinctive, personal style. The paintbrush is an extension of their mind, emotion, and body when they paint. But a camera isn't a

paintbrush, Chaz. Less than a dozen film makers have
ever achieved a truly personal style. Nowadays, it's almost
impossible—the production of a film is a group effort.
To really pull it off, a director must write and film his
own script, do his own editing, do damned near everything by himself. But even then, another indefinable
quality must be added if he wants a personal statement
on film, because everything—almost everything—has been
done already. So if he isn't original, truly original, the
ideas he thinks of as new will probably be derivative.
Blake, at least, was intelligent enough to go back to
early Chinese art for his inspiration. By combining movement to the earlier static forms, he did contribute something cinematically fresh and original.

You still don't follow me?

Well, you aren't an expert, Charlie, that's why. And to
be frank, there are plenty of producers out here who
would've tossed Blake out without a hearing. Not everybody can recognize a personal film style. The distinc-
tion is more subtle than it is in a painting. Here's a
better example; we'll take a checkwriting machine. The
man writing the check holds one pen, and as he signs his
name four more pens also sign his name on four more
checks. A handwriting expert can examine all five signatures and pick out the original signature with no trouble
at all. I mean the one where the checkwriter held the pen.
You and I could look at the five signatures all day long
without seeing any difference in them.

But when it comes to cinema, *I* am an expert. And on
Blake's short twelve-minute film, his personal stamp on
the picture was as obvious to me as the unusual style of
some writer, we'll say, is to you.

Blake knew damned well I'd recognize this quality;
that's why he brought the film along and ran it off for me.

Yes, I hired him, but that was some time later on.

What he really wanted to discuss during that first
meeting was a film script he'd written. It was a beautiful

screenplay; absolutely the finest I've ever read. A wonderful script.

Back in the thirties, Chazz, well before your time, F. Scott Fitzgerald wrote a series of short stories which were published in *Esquire* magazine. They were all of the short-short variety, most of them biter-bit, running from twelve to fifteen hundred words in length. The fictional hero of the series was a broken-down screenwriter named Pat Hobby. This unlikely hero was middle-aged, a drunk, a lousy screenwriter—barely literate, in fact—but the old boy had been around Hollywood for a long time. Once in awhile, out of sentiment, I suppose, for the presound days, some producer would hire Pat Hobby for a week or two at two- or two-fifty a week. Just as a handout, you see. But during the week Hobby held the special writing job, doing additional dialogue or something, the old has-been would dream up some ingenious method to remain on the studio payroll for an extra week or so. That was the gist of most of the tales, anyway; they were clever, but built around this general idea.

Well, J.C. Blake had rediscovered these old Fitzgerald stories. For two full years Jake worked on a feature-length screenplay about Pat Hobby. And by incorporating only the very best of the stories into one ninety-minute script, he'd written one of the cleverest, funniest, and most touching movies I've ever read. The script was a masterpiece. For one thing, there were more than six hundred numbered shots in the script. Ordinarily, feature-lengths rarely run more than three hundred numbered shots—and that's a lot. So you have an idea of how tightly the script was written. But each shot was so well-considered, tying in so well with the next, if two or three shots had been cut out of the script the gaps would've been noticeable.

I must admit that the script had special interest for me. I had met Fitzgerald once or twice in the old days, although I'd forgotten about the old Pat Hobby stories in *Esquire*. But as Blake related some of these stories to me, at lunch, it started me off—reminiscing about the depression days when everything was a hell of a lot more fun out here than it is today.

He left the scenario with me, naturally, and I read it that afternoon and reread it again that night, sitting up at home until after 2 A.M. I simply couldn't get over the labor and the actual man hours Blake had put into the writing. The idea of any screenwriter putting in two full years on the writing of a single screenplay is ridiculous, don't you know. Ben Hecht and Selznick wrote the first half of *Gone With The Wind* in a single weekend —and look what that picture's grossed!

Nevertheless, Charles, new vistas were opened to me. For the first time; no, not really for the first time—I've always had my personal ideas and intimations of what could really be done with cinema. After all, I've been in the business for thirty-six years. But despite the fact that this script of Blake's was a masterpiece of its kind, it was all so damned futile.

You see, if the script had been filmed to the letter, as it was written, the time and the costs would've been fantastic. The editing alone would've taken months. In many of the scenes he not only had the time limit down in seconds, the number of frames were counted! In a way, it was a little frightening; the devotion to detail, I mean. No writer who ever lived—and certainly not Fitzgerald—deserved such dedicated treatment. Not for a movie script—

All I have to do, Chazz, is pick up the phone. Within three minutes I can have three writers in here—or a dozen —all pros, all paid-up guild members. In another five minutes I can block out an ad-libbed movie story of some kind, just a sentence even: "Department store; write a feature-length about employees in an expensive, high-class department store."

The three writers will have a passable shooting script about a department store on my desk within a couple of weeks—the whole bit—theme, main plot, sub-plot, a dual-love story, the works. And it would make a movie, and money would be made. These details are easily worked out by the writers. The script wouldn't be great, but it would be a competent, professional job. In turn, the assigned director studies the script, adds his know-how and skill during the shooting. A couple of stars, with their familiar personalities, and the movie's ready to be scheduled for distribution.

You've written several books, Charles, but let's say now that you're going to write a movie script.

In your description of the hero you'd probably go into considerable detail, wouldn't you? "John Hansen is a personable young man in his late twenties; blond, wavy hair; an infectious smile; tall and broad-shouldered; and yet, he has a boyish quality, an appealing shyness—and so on." That description's off the top of my head, of course, but I could make it as detailed as an inventory of a woman's handbag, and so could you.

But for a screenplay, it would all be wasted effort. Unnecessary writing. A professional screenwriter would only put down three words: "Tab Hunter type."

If the budget were high enough, and if we deemed the story good enough to warrant the dough, we'd even get Tab Hunter to play the role. Why not? On a low-budget, we'd merely cast someone like him. It's easier that way for everybody concerned. When the audience saw Tab Hunter's name on the theater marquee, or in the newspapers, they'd be clued in as to the kind of picture they'd see because he'd be the lead, you see. We've got our audiences trained for typage thinking, and that makes it easier all around for both fans and movie makers. To use another analogy, magazines are the same. A person subscribes to the *Saturday Evening Post* because he knows damned well he's going to reread the same short story every week. If they ran a different kind of a story from the one he was used to every week the poor guy would get nervous, apprehensive—then he'd cancel his subscription. You know this as well as I do. It's basic.

But J.C. Blake . . . He found a simple job that didn't tax his energy too much, night man for a filling station on the Ridge Route, somewhere between here and Bakersfield up in the mountains. He rented an abandoned trapper's cabin, he told me, not too far away from the gas station, and that's where he worked for two years on the screenplay.

Why or how the man got the patience and fortitude is still beyond my comprehension, at least for the writing of a screenplay. They say that James Joyce spent seven years on *Ulysses*, and maybe he did. Well, I'd say that two years' work on one screenplay would be comparable to ten years of work on a novel. Any day.

But when Blake's script was analyzed, as fine as it was, it still boiled down to just another comedy. A fabulous comedy, true enough, but so finely drawn that the average American audience would know whether to laugh or weep. It's the same with Joyce's *Ulysses,* in a way. I've read the book, naturally, and I considered it as an earthy, well-written humorous novel. But D.H. Lawrence, of all people, called it a *dirty* book. And then, we have the scholarly types. Did you know that there's a quarterly magazine that's been published for many years now called *The James Joyce Review*? That may not be the exact title, but it's similar to that. And in every quarterly issue scholars are still finding new things to write about *Ulysses* and other Joycean writings. After all these years.

Who, for God's sake, could ever take movies that seriously? Or any one movie?

Now you follow me. Jake Blake did. Right.

Well, when you read the run-of-the-mill scripts I get in here day after day, it was a curious pleasure for me to read a script like his. Honest to Jesus, Charlie, some of the scripts sent in were written for other shows and other studios, and then rejected. And when I get them, the agents and writers are too damned lazy to rewrite another title page to fit any of my shows. This happens all the time.

Disregarding technical work, Blake's major mistake was this, although he must've made the mistake deliberately. In a comedy, let's say, especially in a comedy, the hero must be likeable. The audience can laugh at him or with him, but they must like him well enough to want him to come out on top in the end. This is a tricky bit, particularly if the guy is one of those stupid, ineffectual comics. In this case, we don't often let the comic get the girl—unless she's the same stupid type—because even though the audience likes the hero, they have a tendency to feel sorry for the girl who gets stuck in a marriage with some sap, you see.

This may sound like hair-splitting, but it isn't. No matter how well the audience *likes* the hero, they can never be allowed to really *care* about the things that happen to him. This was Charlie Chaplin's secret. People liked him all right, but he saw to it by his makeup and ridiculous costume that people would never believe that the on-screen personage was a real person. He was always a character, and the fact that he could jerk tears and laughter both out of an audience as a character was only due to the period of suspended belief during the running time of the movie.

Please, don't let me get off on the genius of Chaplin—

In Fitzgerald's Pat Hobby stories, no one could really identify themselves with the character. The readers, I suppose, enjoyed the stories because they liked to see an ignorant person outmaneuver a big shot.

Blake's Pat Hobby had an extra dimension, although he was basically the same character Fitzgerald created. Can you read a script and see it on the screen as you read it? I can. An audience would've *cared* about Pat Hobby on the screen. When you really love someone, you can't laugh when he gets hurt. Pat Hobby was a drunk and a failure—funny, yes, but pathetically so. If you have an enemy, and he becomes an alcoholic, it's human nature to rejoice to a certain extent at his downfall. But you can't laugh at any alcoholic, no matter how funny the things are that he does, if he's a member of your immediate family.

This was a special type of movie, a beautiful screenplay, and it's a shame it was never filmed. Blake overdid it; the characterization was too good.

And the way it was written, it was mandatory that an unknown actor had to play the part of Hobby. Any well-known actor, with his image impressed indelibly on the mass-audience mind through dozens of movie exposures, would've completely spoiled the script. Blake had planned it that way.

No, it makes no difference how great the actor is; in movies the audience has the actor and the character fused. So you see the problem. Chaplin and his screen character were one, and no matter how emotionally involved the audience became during one of his movies, when they left the theater they knew that Chaplin was actually a millionaire living in Hollywood. It's the system, Charlie.

Hell, yes, I bought the script! I'd have been a fool not to—somebody else would've grabbed it. I called Blake's agent the next morning and paid five thousand dollars for it—although I probably could've got it for less.

At the time there was considerable public interest in Fitzgerald. They had done a ninety-minute TV play about then, an adaptation of his unfinished novel, *The Last Tycoon*. And Fitzgerald's former mistress had written an "as told to" book about their shacking up days out here. She must've really hated his guts to publish that sordid book; it was in poor taste, to say the least. But even the staid old publishing firm of Scribner's had begun to reissue Fitzgerald's old novels in quality-type paperbacks, so Blake's screenplay was a good property. I bought it, and had it registered.

A few months later, as I said, I hired Blake as a director. I needed a replacement director for the series we were filming then called *City Block*. We shot three fifteen-minute scripts every week for sale to independent stations. They could be used as morning or afternoon filler; it was strictly daytime stuff. For variety we had about fifty actors on a roster for this series, but the three directors—one for each show—were semipermanent. Every Friday we mailed out sides, not complete scripts, to the actors we'd need for the three plays the next week. They learned their lines at home, and when they reported to the studio the director gave them a couple of runthroughs and then put the play on film. It was only a fifteen-minute daytime show, and most directors were off the set by noon.

But Blake took all day, and sometimes went into overtime. Here's the deal—most of the actors had never seen each other before; they didn't even know the plot of the story, because they only had their own parts and cue lines. But Blake still wanted to lecture them about motivation and all that stuff, and some of these people had other shows to do in the afternoon and in the evening. There were conflicts, you see, and in addition to overtime, the spontaneity of the barely rehearsed actors was the only thing that gave any life to the substandard scripts. Blake got the actors to thinking, emoting, and the scripts couldn't stand it. There's a time to shoot the works and a time to be practical. I had to let him go.

It wasn't long after he left us when he did a color Western for one of the independents. One reliable rumor has it that he ran them eight hundred thousand bucks over the budget. If you cut that in half, which is closer to the truth, it's still a goodly sum. It was a good Western, but after all, Chazz, what can anybody do with a Western? It was cleverly done for an oater, but a Western in color is merely a Western that isn't in black-and-white.

After that Jake drifted back East for a year or so, and picked up financial backing for a version of *Everyman* he'd written. He did the play in Middle English, too, so it was a critical success. Those college professor critics who do New York reviews eat that stuff up, but it flopped at the box office. New York audiences don't even understand good English, let alone Middle English.

But Mammoth bought the script anyway, and brought J.C. out here to direct. The movie didn't break even in the U.S., but an odd thing happened. He filmed the movie the way the old morality plays were originally staged in England during the seventeenth century. Each scene was performed on a different wagon, and these plays were put on at fairs. When a scene was done the wagon moved on to another waiting group of spectators and the next wagon and the next scene pulled in. The technique was so old it almost seemed fresh, and because his budget was low, J.C. shot the movie with unknown actors.

But here's what's funny. It flopped in the U.S., but for some reason the movie really appealed to Latin Americans. *Everyman,* with Spanish subtitles, has been running for several years now to a packed house in Mexico City. It's the same story in Spain and other South American countries, and Mammoth actually made some fair money on the film.

Why? Well, I don't know if it's true or not, but according to one theory the Mexicans and other Spanish-speaking people think the movie is in Basic English instead of Middle English. The same people go again and again to see it, so it's believed that they're trying to learn how to speak English from the film. Odd, isn't it?

Yes, of course. Blake made more movies. He did a mystery and at least two more oaters, plus some others.

And I hired him to direct an hour-long special, *Roller-Skating, U.S.A.* He also directed a television series called *Camp Cook*. This was supposed to be a nonviolent type of Western for children; a stupid idea that was doomed before it even started. But J.C.'s been working right along, and he finally got a reputation as a good, competent director—as a man who knows his job. It simply doesn't make any sense for a man as talented as J.C. Blake to slice his wrists—

The old Pat Hobby scenario?

Yeah, I finally used it; that is, I managed to salvage a lot of good bits and pieces out of the script. I put two contract writers on it and they turned the script into a thirteen-week series.

We junked the middle-aged screenwriter character. We named the show *The Man and The Method*. We changed the drunken screenwriter to struggling young actor here in Hollywood. Instead of a writer trying to get studio writing jobs, the young actor tried to get various TV parts every week. And he always got the part he wanted each week by pulling some clever ruse or working out a gimmick of some kind. Audience response was excellent, especially from teen-agers. We had a little sponsor trouble, but otherwise we could've had at least two seasons out of the series. It goes into reruns in 1964.

But I'm tired of talking, Charlie. About the business, even about myself—at least for today. I'll be all right again tomorrow. It's just that—well, when a brilliant man like J.C. Blake cuts his wrists, you sometimes wonder what in the hell the whole damned business is all about. That's all.

Thank *you,* for coming in . . .

A LETTER TO A.A. (ALMOST ANYBODY)

Dear sir,

or maybe you're a lady, or a disparate group—I don't know. I am an alcoholic, or should that be capitalized? All right. I make you a gift of the Capital. I am an Alcoholic, and I need your help. At least I think I do; I'm not sure. I'm not sure of anything anymore except that I am an Alcoholic, and a sober one at that; and if there is anything more disgusting than a sober alc—pardon— *Alcoholic,* I don't know what it is. Being sober all the time has me befuddled and confused, although up to now I was under the impression that being sober was supposed to be an ideal—or at least idealistic—state for an Alcoholic. I know I feel better even though I feel worse, and if you can make good sense out of that then you are a better man, or a woman, or an Alcoholic than I am.

"Talk it out, George,·that's the only way to get at the roots of the thing." That's what Fred; he's the chairman at our local A.A. chapter, and that's what Fred—I never asked him what his last name was, although I know what it is, and he never asked for mine although he knew it—but you know the rules about last names as well as I do, and all I'm trying to do now is follow Fred's advice as he said I ought to do: Talk it out, George!

Down to it, get down to it—I keep trying to delay, to put it off, to sneak around it and avoid the over, under, or through; I even went back and read my last paragraph. Like Faulkner, man, *sir,* I mean, and now I know how he wrote all of those compounded and involved syntaxes—he was sober, he had to be. But I'll start, and if the beginning doesn't make me reach for that brown unopened bottle in front of me nothing else will, or so I think but really don't know. I do know, or think I know, that by the time I finish this letter, or scream, if I can finish it, and if you get it, which you will, I suppose, if I mail it, and I'll mail it if I can find a stamp around the house some place, and if you *do* get it, which you will if it is delivered, my problem will be solved long before then. Mr. Anthony, I have a problem—what ever became of Mr. Anthony, anyway?

All right. The beginning. If I don't weep, and maybe this time I won't; isn't it possible that the time will come when the beginning will no longer make a man cry? Don't the tears ever dry up and go away somewhere? Like how many times does a man have to pay for it? I mean the beginning, and I was drunk even then, although I wasn't then a drunk—an Alcoholic. I became a drunk—an Alcoholic—because I was drunk at the time. And because I was drunk at the time, that's how it happened, although I wasn't an *Alcoholic* at the time; I was only drunk, which isn't the same, as you know.

My wife's arm.

Some, several minutes have gone by, fifteen of them maybe. I smoked a cigarette, taking my time; I didn't open the bottle, and I didn't weep. A milestone. This is the first time for this test, the written test, and I was able to think about *it* without trying to drown it, or *pickle* it is a better term, although drinking never really worked anyway.

My wife's arm. There; it was much easier to write the second time. Arm. Arm, arm, arm, arm, arm. Nothing, none.

Maybe I'm finished inside, all gone, empty, voided, like my wife's arm. It is gone and I did it and I'm an Alcoholic, a sober Alcoholic right now, but I was one of the drunkest Alcoholics anybody ever saw around this town for the last four years. And even though this is a small city, there have been some mighty fine drunks residing here, including my friend Fred before *he* sobered up and then did the same for me. I drank with the best of them, boy, I mean, sir (madame?), although later on I preferred to drink alone; that is, around the house where I could see her, because she never touched a drop after— My wife, and her arm—or where the arm used to be. It sort of kept the evil spirits up—no *double entendre* intended—I'm not trying to be funny, for God's sake, I'm trying to get down to it.

The accident, and my wife's arm. (And how can I tell about it without sounding like a lugubrious, fatuous ass?) Although, if I hadn't been drunk at the time—I said this—there wouldn't have been any accident and my wife would still have her arm. Her left arm; that's the arm that was "sheared off at the shoulder," as the newspaper reported it. Sheared off; the car door did it, but I really did it because I was drunk at the time and driving home from the country club dance, recklessly—the same old monotonous Saturday night dance that is held every Saturday night during the summer—outside on the patio when the weather's nice (with Japanese lanterns), and inside when it rains, and maybe the dances are still being held. I never went back to the club again, not after the accident. I was too afraid that somebody would commiserate with me, or worse, pretend to talk about something else while they were really thinking about my wife's lost arm and me drunk and smashing up the car. And I didn't even get a scratch, not a scratch.

I was *lucky*, my mother told me, even as she was bawling, and dead now (she died, Mother, eight months after the accident, the old liver trouble she had had for years, poor sweet soul), but in that dismal, horrible, gray Sunday dawn at the hospital—and I was sober *then*, all right, hanging around first in the hall and then in the waiting room and back to the hall, unable to sit down, not even for a second, the beard stubble on my face making me feel dirty, and the damned cigarette machine in the corridor only took a quarter and a nickel, not three dimes, and nobody had any change, of course, and my mother picked this time to say, crying, "You were lucky, George."

"Lucky!" The strangled scream hurt my throat, and then the doctor came and I was crying wildly and carrying on, hitting the innocent white walls with my fists; and he gave me a shot that didn't work and told me to go home.

Not me. I went to the White Springs Hotel instead and bought two fifths of Old Grandpappy from the night bellhop. Even *before* I became an Alcoholic I had the professional Alcoholic's cunning instinct for knowing when, where, and how to get a needed bottle or so when the bars and package stores were closed. Those two bottles and a good many more saw me through during the days before my wife came home from the hospital—minus her arm.

And I visited her every single day, trying to get the precise, exact balance into my system so I'd have enough of the magic fluid inside me to get me there—to the hospital—and into Louise's private room, and not too much so she would notice any effects on me, but I *never* did get the perfect balance, or enough inside me not to notice that her arm wasn't there anymore. And each time, before I left home to go to the hospital, I'd say to myself, "Now this time, don't look! Look into her bright, bright eyes, or simply read to her from a book, or look at the floor and count the cracks and wet-mop marks, or look at the table, the bedspread, or even the new red scar on her temple, but don't look at her arm!"

But the moment I entered Louise's room, trying to smile, trying to say something cheerful, and most of the time struggling to say just something, anything, my eyes couldn't keep away from that— I could never stay put for the full two-hour visiting period without excusing myself and going to the men's room down the hall for a drink. I always stashed a bottle in there before going to my wife's room; just plain old common horse-sense (the kind that convinces us that the world is flat), because I never would have made it otherwise, unless— I think I could have taken it a little better, perhaps, if Louise had only berated me, cursed me. This idea is only supposition, but Louise took it too well, too bravely, like a saint. And she lost so much weight so fast she even looked like a saint, too. There was always the touch of pink on her lips, the lipstick a little crooked; awkwardly applied, of course, the pitiful *effort* to fix-herself-up for my daily visit. And the too-too sweet martyr's smile, and the round wet eyes, wet, but without tears. No bitterness, ever, never a whimper out of her, not a word about its being all my fault. There's a Christian for you, every damned time.

But that's enough about the beginning, and all that, but it led to later, much later, some four years later when everything was gone, my business, at least my half of it; I sold out at less than a tenth of what my half was worth because I had to have the cash. (I was a public accountant, not a C.P.A., but we were doing all right, Herb and I, counting the increased income tax business and all; and Herb got up the price I asked for my half because I had set it so deliberately and ridiculously low. All was fair, and I have no complaints on that score. I certainly wasn't pulling my share of the load; after the accident I didn't go to the office more than once or twice a week. And then I didn't go at all because I couldn't do any work if I did go; for more than a year before I sold out to Herb I didn't set foot in the place. I just phoned and asked Herb to call the bank and okay a ten or a twenty-dollar check for me when I needed dough. And when Herb came to his senses and refused to okay any more checks for me, I sold out to him— and that money went, too.)

The money all went so fast. The hospital bills. The doctors. I couldn't afford the private room for Louise in the first place, but I couldn't afford *not* to have it; or the exorbitant, accompanying medical consultations, which were nothing but money thrown down the drain. The savings, the bonds all went (there were the expensive private "rehabilitation" lessons for my wife), and then our home went, too. The car, of course, was a total loss; I used the insurance money as one of the hospital payments. And Mother died, and I had to pay for her funeral. Although Mother didn't have any money of her own, I inherited her tiny house, naturally, which was fortuitous, if it was anything. Louise and I moved into it, and here we were:

Louise, with only one arm, was making like a housewife, and I was making like a drunk with both of my arms, and there was no money coming in—suddenly, just like that, we were on Relief! The bounty of the County. But I didn't really care, not at first—at least Mother never lived to see the Day—she *would* have cared. All at once we were on the "poor and needy" rolls of all the weird churches and women's clubs in the city. The Methodists, the Baptists, the Church of God's Flock, the Presbyterians, and naturally, the Unitarians took this *avid* interest in our affairs. The Unitarians were in on it because of *Mother,* and all of the ministers from these various churches kept coming around to commiserate with my wife. A new one every day, it seemed, and my wife and the visiting minister would be kneeling and praying and talking in undertones by the hour in the living room while I sat in the kitchen trying to drown their funereal voices with a bottle. *Tres gai,* it was, but I couldn't say anything about it, one way or the other, because this sort of thing was all the pleasure my wife had left to her—evidently; she couldn't talk to me, and I couldn't talk to her—

The social worker's name was Miss Whiteside. Mary

Ellen Whiteside. She was about thirty-two, give a few years, and her weekly visits to the house with the weekly check were like clockwork. Miss Whiteside didn't resemble the social worker stereotype, except perhaps for her absurd hats and white gloves, and she drove a Buick, not last year's Ford or Chevvy like most of them drive. But she was right there with the fifty-five dollar check every week, on time, and in person. With Alcoholics, the social worker is required to bring the weekly check in person instead of mailing them (only idiots, imbeciles and morons are entitled to get their relief checks via the mails). Alcoholics can't be trusted, it seems. Miss Whiteside would hand me the check, and after I signed it she pointedly handed it to my wife—another rule—and then departed in her baby-blue Buick. My good wife, who now walked a little lopsided, despite the expensive rehabilitation lessons, would then trot down to the corner, cash the check, and bring the money—all of it—back to me. I would give Louise ten or fifteen magnanimous dollars, and drink through the rest of it. Oh, my wife never said a word about my drinking—not to me, anyway—the martyr bit, don't you know. I think it was Shaw who said something about martyrs, that martyrdom is the way to recognition for the person of no talent or ability—something like that—the exact quotation doesn't make any difference.

If we had only fought, or talked things over "sensibly," or if she had only screamed her head off at me, piling enough curses on my head to enable me to desert the woman in all good conscience, but no; it was always pretend, pretend, pretend. Everything is lovely. Of course, her arm was gone, and she had an unsightly four-inch scar on her forehead, as well as the jagged scar on her temple, and she had dropped from a well-shaped 120 pounds down to a scrawny eighty-six pounds (the arm hadn't weighed that much!), and me, her blottery husband—I was a drunk, my business was gone, my money was gone, our beautiful home was gone, and we were on Relief.

Relief. Daily, the churches delivered food baskets to our door. We had no children, but that didn't make any difference—we got toys delivered to the house just the same. Ladies' clubs and auxiliaries were driving up in groups and depositing clothes, dresses, suits, shirts, shoes, and all kinds of stuff on our front porch. Last Christmas, for example, we got six basketfuls of assorted groceries, three turkeys—one of them already cooked and stuffed —and two Christmas trees, complete with ornaments, delivered right to the door by these good, God-fearing people.

Oh, no, nothing was wrong. Nothing had happened, the way Louise and I acted toward each other, so very polite and all—we accepted all of this stuff with mumbled thanks to the donors as though it were the way people were supposed to live. We didn't sleep together anymore —that sort of thing would have been impossible for me— and Louise never mentioned it.

So I would drink up the money at Nelson's, the bar nearest to the house, setting them up for the boys when I had the cash (after rat-holing some of my weekly stipend first for package stuff later in the week); and after the money was gone I pawned some of the clothing the women's clubs and auxiliaries brought around for the purpose. And so it all went until Fred managed to get through to me and straightened me out.

Fred was an Alcoholic, he said, and it was time that I, too, recognized the fact that I was an Alcoholic.

"Okay," I said, "so I'm an Alcoholic."

"So we talk it out," Fred said.

And talk it out I did, as well as I could, although I had reached the point where I didn't care whether I was an Alcoholic or not—or so I thought. I couldn't talk to my disabled wife, and Fred didn't judge me; he was easy to talk to, after I got started. We attended A.A. meetings together, although I went to these meetings as a favor to Fred, at first. Sitting there that way, in the rented hall, listening to those people—Alcoholics like myself—and hearing some of the terrible stories they told which were worse than mine—well, perhaps not. No man ever has troubles that are greater than another man's, but these stories were sort of inspiring to me: comebacks had been made, after all; and almost overnight, it seemed, I quit drinking. I didn't taper off, I merely quit, just like that, and just for a day at a time, as Fred had suggested. And it was easy because I knew it was only for the day, and I could start drinking the next morning if I wanted to—but I didn't. I began to get a few friendly, encouraging visits from other A.A. members, and they were all decent guys . . .

It took about a month. I was fairly well straightened out, but I was restless. A man has to do something, and I wasn't doing anything because I had lost my fulltime job of drinking. I started thinking about a job. Naturally, I didn't go back and see old Herb, or try for anything in the accounting line. I wasn't ready yet; too many people around town knew that I was a drunk; and I wasn't about to put any of my former friends on the spot by forcing them to turn me down for a job. But there was a brand new supermarket that had opened recently only six blocks away from the house, and I applied there for a position, talking frankly to the manager.

"I'm an Alcoholic," I told him bluntly, "but I've joined A.A., and I haven't had a drink now for more than a month. I need a job, and I have to get my self-respect back. I know figures, I'm a competent accountant, and if you'll give me a chance I can mark prices on cans, total inventories for you, and—"

"Grab a broom," he said.

The manager gave me a chance, and thirty-five dollars a week. I was issued a black leather bow tie, a clean apron, and a new broom. There were tears of gratitude in my eyes; I could have kissed his feet, then and there . . .

And all week long I've been working—sweeping, dusting, mopping, carrying—and shivering happily in the frigid air-conditioning of the new store.

Miss Whiteside came around this afternoon, on my first day off, with the weekly relief check. I laughed; with the excitement and all, I had forgotten to telephone her about my new job.

"I've got a job, Miss Whiteside," I said proudly. I tore the relief check in half, and handed her the pieces.

She flushed slightly, started to say something, but my wife caught her eye. The two women went outside and sat, talking, in Miss Whiteside's car for about twenty minutes; and then the social worker drove away, for what I thought was the last time. But it was just a few minutes ago, before I started to write this letter, when Miss Whiteside returned. After my wife let her in and retired behind the closed door of her bedroom, Miss Whiteside placed a fifth of whiskey on the kitchen table before me.

"Let's talk for awhile, George," Miss Whiteside began, favoring me with a friendly smile. "For once in your life, I think you should think about somebody else instead of yourself."

"What—?"

"Please, let me talk." She placed a white-gloved hand on my arm. "You, George, are an Alcoholic. You know it and I know it, so why pretend that you aren't?"

"Who's pretending?" I protested.

"You are, George. You won't keep that sweeper's job for two weeks, and in your heart you know it. You can't possibly keep away from liquor, George, because you're an Alcoholic. Besides, what are they paying you? Thirty-five dollars a week. We're already paying you fifty-five dollars a week, so what do you think you're gaining by pretending to be something you're not? And if you don't have any feelings left for your poor crippled wife, who'll be cut off from every organized charity in town the moment it gets around that you're working again, what about me?"

"You?"

"Haven't I been decent to you ever since I took your case? Did I ever lecture you, bawl you out for drinking?"

"No." I shook my head.

"Have I ever been late with your check? Have I ever asked for a kickback?"

"No," I replied defensively. "But I'm entitled to some credit myself. I've always been here to sign it when you came, whether I've been drunk or sober!"

"Granted. And don't think I haven't appreciated it either, George. But for a moment, just for a moment, I want you to hear my side of the story. Do you know that there are only thirty-two cases left on the county relief rolls? The truth of the matter is, George, I'm already in trouble. If I don't come up with at least two or three more active cases by the beginning of the fiscal year I'm liable to lose my job—or at best, be transferred into the city. And I've got my roots here, George. I support my mother, and it isn't easy to find new social worker positions nowadays—not in these prosperous times," she added bitterly. To my astonishment her lips trembled, but before I could say anything she went ahead with it. "The truth of the matter is this, George: I need you on my rolls, and you and your wife need me. So for once in your life, show a little selflessness. You want a drink right now, don't you?" She pushed the bottle toward me.

"No," I said honestly, "I really don't want a drink, Miss Whiteside. One drink would probably get me started all over again. But I honestly didn't know that the times were so good—I mean, so *bad,* from your point of view."

"It so happens that they are, George." She sighed. The corners of her worried mouth turned up slightly, but it wasn't even a good imitation of a brave smile; and her eyes behind her glasses were much too bright.

"I know you won't let me down, George." She touched me lightly, timidly, on the shoulder. "Or your poor wife, either." She turned away, and smoothed the skirt wrinkles down over her hips. "I'll leave the bottle," she added, without looking back.

For a long time after Miss Whiteside left the house I just sat here at the table, staring bewilderedly at the bottle of whiskey without really seeing it, and then I began to write this long, desperate—yes, what else?—meaningless letter. And now that I've finished it I'm going to open the bottle and have a small drink, and then, perhaps another. Why not? When next Christmas rolls around, maybe we'll get *eight* lousy turkeys—

Nobody's,
I Am an Alcoholic

JAKE'S JOURNAL

First Entry (Undated)

THIS LEDGER and more than two dozen ballpoint pens
have all been here in the tower for a long time. I do
not know why I did not start a journal, or diary, long
before now. If I had started in the beginning I might
have been able to at least put down the date. Not that
I have a great deal to relate since this assignment, but I
have had lately a suspicion (a slight one to be sure), that
all is not right here. And a certain evilness is beginning
to make itself felt in the atmosphere. As my mind comes
close to perceiving what I believe, in time, will be a
complete revelation of everything, the thought slips away
from me, like a dark cloud merging with another cloud,
and I am further away from the truth than before. But
then, I am not really surprised. Very few men know the
answers to anything, much less everything.

· I will begin with a description of my surroundings. I
know this dark field better now than I know the streets
of Los Angeles, my home town. But writing this way, putting the image of this place into words, is as good a way
to start as any I can think of, and if writing helps to pass
the time, that in itself is a fair reward.

There are no maps in the tower, so I cannot place
the geographical location with any exactness. I believe
this auxiliary landing field lies somewhere in Tibet, although I am not even certain of that. As yet I have not
seen a native of the place, and before a native could get
to this field he would have to fly in by airplane like I did.

I do not believe it would be possible to climb, on foot, the terrible mountains we flew over to reach this field, although I have hoped innumerable times that someone, anyone, would come stumbling down the snowy mountainside to this lonely tower.

The field is not a large one. The strip is not much larger than a football field. The surface of the landing strip is made of crushed black stones. These glistening stones are peculiar in that they are warm to the touch. Not hot, but warm, warm enough to melt the everfalling snow as it touches the field. As I look out from the tower now, in the black night, the field shines like an onyx lake. The lake is surrounded on all sides by high, clean banks of snow, terraced back naturally by the wind to the four jagged mountain peaks pointing at the field. Due west is a kind of a pass and the only decent approach to the field by airplane. When the pilot dropped me off here he must have landed from that direction. And if another airplane ever lands here, it will also have to come in from the west. I am not a pilot, and perhaps it might be possible to glide down one of these sheer mountains by barely skimming along the surface if the wind was not blowing. But the wind is always blowing. Since I have been stationed here the wind has always blown with great force straight from the pass, causing a sharp, steep updraft which would surely cause any airplane to crash if it attempted to fly down and into the field.

Perhaps a helicopter could make it.

Along the edges of the field there are little red and green lights spaced four thirty-inch steps apart.

Squaring the field, the lights are alternated, red-green, red-green, all of the way around. There is also a small searchlight atop the tower that circles once around every sixty seconds. That is my job: I replace the bulbs as they burn out. When it gets dark I turn on the field lights and the searchlight. In the morning I turn them off. Not much of a job, but I make the square of the field once a day looking for bulbs that have burned out. The temperature is considerably below zero and I am always glad to get back to the tower. In addition to these simple maintenance duties I am also supposed to service any airplane forced to land here. There are several hundred drums of fuel lining the field and I do not know how many more buried under the snow behind the tower for this purpose. So far, no airplane has landed. Whoever it was who planned this emergency field greatly over-estimated the air traffic. Although I am only a Basic Air-man, I am certain the government is wasting their money by keeping me here. Not that I have been paid in all of the months I have been here, and even if I were paid, I do not know how I could spend my money.

The tower itself is not large. The downstairs part has two storerooms in addition to my sleeping-living room. Right above my bedroom, where I am writing this, is this glassed-in tower room. In the tower is this broad metal desk which takes in the entire front window over-looking the field. The other three sides are filled with radio equipment. None of it works. During the first few months I was here I fiddled and worked with the radio equipment for hours with no results. I do not know any-thing about electronics, but I do know that none of the stuff up here works. In the center of the floor there is a hole and a wooden ladder to the downstairs room. The downstairs room contains my wooden bunk, a gasoline stove, a chair, and a wardrobe made out of a packing-case where I keep my uniforms. That is another thing that irritates me. Coming here from the Philippine Islands like I did, all I had were cotton khaki uniforms. They should have issued me woolen uniforms for Tibet. If it were not for the dirty sheepskin jacket left here by the previous custodian I do not know how I would make my daily rounds of the field without freezing to death.

The two storerooms each have a door into my sleeping

room. The door to the outside is made of heavy oak. One of the storerooms contains my provisions and the other has nothing in it except electric light bulbs. The provisions allow for no variety in meal planning. One side of the storeroom is piled high with canned Argentine corned beef, and the other side is stacked to the ceiling with one hundred pound sacks of small, white dried beans. This is a rotten diet for a man, and whoever provisioned this tower should have thought to lay in a supply of coffee. I drink hot water instead, and although it warms my stomach, it is a poor substitute for coffee.

About thirty yards away from the tower is the shed with the generator and the two-cylinder gasoline engine for the field and tower lights. That is about it. No books, no radio, no magazines, and no company. How the Air Force ever expected a man to be contented in a place like this is beyond me.

This is enough for the first entry. My fingers are a bit cramped, not being used to writing, although I did enjoy writing this down. I wish, now, that I had thought of it sooner.

Second Entry (Undated)

JUST BEFORE STARTING this entry I reread the first one and found it pleasant to have something to read. It isn't strange to read something you wrote yourself and I wouldn't be surprised if writers themselves didn't go back and read their own books over and over. Inasmuch as I have nothing to read except what I write myself it will be better and better the more I put down. In time when I get a lot written I can go back and by merely reading what I've put down I can kill several hours at a time. Considering that, it will pay me to write as well as I can.

Being alone as I have for so long now that I hesitate to guess, and with little to do, my mind takes a lot of strange journeys. This morning I was thinking of books, and I thought I should have brought at least one book along with me. This in turn led me to think, "What book?" Such speculation can kill a lot of time. I tried my best to remember all the books I've read, going back to when I first started with *The Little Red Hen;* and although I left out a lot of them, surely, I ended up thinking about the last one I read, or one of the last, *Look Homeward, Angel,* by Thomas Wolfe. The latter was read at the insistence of Red Galvin, my onetime bunkmate at Pampanga, because he said it was good. I didn't think so because there wasn't much plot to it and was mostly about a common Southern family. But as Galvin said, it was funny, and for a place like this, with just one good book, if I had it, it would be good because it was thick. Thickness in books made me think of the Bible. I remembered a magazine piece where several people were asked what book they considered the most valuable to have in their library, and about eight out of ten of them said, the Bible. I've never read the Bible, although I've skimmed through it a few times, and I won one once at Sunday School for memorizing a few pet phrases of our teacher's. I wouldn't, if I had a choice, bring a Bible here, but I'd settle for almost any thick book.

Then I thought about music. In Pampanga, when I was living with Elena Espeneida, I had a small wind-up phonograph and two records. One was a Bing Crosby and the other was *Afternoon of a Faun,* parts one and two. I enjoyed both of those records very much. After I taught Elena how to work the phonograph she played them over and over for me. She was partial to the second part of *Afternoon of a Faun* but she also liked the Bing Crosby record. I guess she still has the phonograph and the two records. I like to think that as she plays them now she thinks of me. In fact I *know* she must think of me every time she plays them. And as much as I would like to have that phonograph and the two records here, I wouldn't deprive Elena of them. I was the only decent thing that ever happened to that girl and I would never destroy her wonderful memories of me.

The whole affair with Elena was a strange one. My memories of her are sweet and sad, leaving a taste like burned bacon in my mouth as I recall the termination of that affair.

I was driving the fire truck those days. This left me free time every other morning when the rest of the squadron was working and I took advantage of it.

Two miles away from the field was the little *barrio* of Sapang Bato which we used to call Sloppy Bottom. I don't know why it was called that. Maybe Sapang Bato means Sloppy Bottom in English. On the edge of this little *barrio*, the fringe, was the Air Force Settlement. This was a group of eight or ten shacks rented by wealthier airmen like sergeants and enlisted crew members on flying pay. In the shacks they installed their Filipino women, their house furnishings, and their demijohns of gin and rum. To a Basic Airman like myself, these women were fair prey. Knowing they were available but difficult to be had, I spent several weeks in thought before finding a solution that worked; a plan that would get me into the houses when none of their men were around. Although most of these women were passed on to another NCO when a man left for the States, there was a lot of talk (by the men who paid the rent and girl) about how faithful their girls were and how well they could be trusted. Of course, the more money, clothes, candy and PX items they gave their girls, the more faithful they were. But there were some of the stingier sergeants who thought their girls would be faithful on the most minimum kind of allowance; thinking in their stupid way that the girls "loved" them. The more stupid the man is the happier he is, it seems.

"Honeymoon Lotion" proved to be the solution to my problem. This was a milky-white fluid in a green bottle sold exclusively in the Hindu's Gift Shop. Contents were one litre, which is about a fifth of a gallon. This lotion smelled malodorous to an American nose. It was an unpleasant mixture of coconut oil, wintergreen, burnt sugar and I don't know what all. Filipino girls, however, loved the smell of it. They used "Honeymoon Lotion" on their hair; they rubbed it on their bodies; and when it was used in large enough amounts it covered the fact they hadn't bathed recently. It made their brown skins shine with the oily shine of a fish stinking in the moonlight. They loved it. It only cost one peso, and I had credit with the Hindu.

It was on a morning off that I met Elena. I had a bottle of "Honeymoon Lotion" in my hand, and had walked the two miles from the barracks to the *barrio*, taking the shortcut through the Baluga village. My plan was simple and foolproof. I usually went directly to the Air Force Settlement swinging the green bottle in my hand. The girls would watch me from the porches of their stilted shacks. Sooner or later one of the girls would engage me in conversation. We would then go inside for a drink of her man's gin or rum. I would engage the girl in promiscuous intercourse and then depart. I always left behind the bottle of "Honeymoon Lotion." I didn't mind the smell, but I know that several sergeants were bitter about it when they got home from the base, wondering where the women got the lotion.

But this particular morning, I had paused at the well which was centrally located in the *barrio*. A slender girl was filling her five-gallon Standard Oil can with water. I thought she was beautiful and wondered how I had missed seeing her before. She was young and appeared to be shy. Her upper lip was beaded slightly with perspiration and her skin was the color of buttered toast that has been made just right. In the early sunshine she glistened and her thick black hair was a plaited rope hanging down her back. She was barefooted and she wore a faded blue dress.

I caught the sun with my bottle and the reflection put a greenish light on her face. She paid no attention, and I moved in closer.

I cleared my throat almost in her ear. She was startled and stepped back, her chin on her chest. She said nothing and kept her eyes looking down at the ground. I raised her chin with my hand and looked into her eyes. She was blind. It was like looking into two almond-sized pools of cream.

"I didn't mean to frighten you," I said. "I admired your beauty so much I was trying to start a conversation."

"I didn't know anyone was watching me. But I wasn't frightened."

"I wasn't watching you. I was staring, but I didn't know you were blind."

"I must go home." She smiled. Her voice was tiny; it was the voice of a princess in an animated cartoon. She would have lifted her can of water but I took it away from her.

"Go on home. I'll carry it for you." She hesitated a moment, then surefooted and confidently she led the way through rubbish-laden back alleys, in and out of yard-ways, and up a deadend dirt street to the house at the end of it. The little house was on stilts like the rest of the *barrio* houses, and she stopped beneath the ladder.

"I live here." She pointed directly above her head to the hole in the floor that was used as a door. I marveled at her ability to walk unerringly to her house as I put the can of water on the ground.

"Are you sure this is your house?" I asked.

"Oh, yes!" She laughed girlishly and I had to join in. It was that kind of a laugh.

At this moment an old man stuck his head through the hole and started spouting in Tagalog. The girl climbed swiftly up the ladder and inside. The old man clambered down; his face was dark red with rage.

"Go away! You keep away from here! Elena is blind girl. No good for you!" He shook his little fist in my face.

"Take it easy, Papasan," I said. "Nobody's going to hurt your little girl." I twisted his arm behind his back and flung him into a nearby bush. He was up in an instant; his eyes were like shiny, black marbles. Then, probably realizing the futility of it all, he began to cry.

"You just take it easy, Pop," I told him. I lighted two cigarettes and gave him one. He started to smoke it, and calmed down. "You can't hide a girl like that forever, Pop. They grow up on you. I'll be back tonight."

I whistled and the girl stuck her head through the hole. I climbed the ladder and put the bottle of "Honeymoon Lotion" in her hand.

"I'll be back tonight," I said and dropped to the ground. I patted the old man on the shoulder and left.

That night I went back. I gave the old man several sacks of tobacco and some cigarette papers. I took the girl before I left. I was happy with her and spent several weeks at the little house. I often stayed all night and on most of my free weekends. I bought her the phonograph, on credit from the Hindu, and the two records. It was refreshing to have a girl like Elena after the hard-bitten professional girls who lived with the sergeants.

The breakup came as a surprise, even though I should have seen it coming. The airmen at Pampanga were so stupid I could hardly speak to them. I had one friend, Red Galvin, at the time, and when I wanted to talk to someone I talked to him. It was my own fault for not realizing that my little deal with Elena would cause vicious jealousy.

I'd been drinking gin in the shack and talking to Elena until almost midnight. She had fanned me, as I talked, with a palm leaf and it had been an enjoyable evening. Instead of staying the night I decided to go back to the barracks.

I cut through the Baluga village and was on the trail that led across the plain when I was jumped by three men. Ducky Halpert, Vernon Watson and Melvin Powell were the three. Between them they worked me over pretty well. I got in a few good licks, of course, but the viciousness of their attack caught me by surprise and I took quite a beating. After I was down, and after I was kicked a few times I said I'd had enough. They let me up and the night was quiet except for the heavy breathing all of us were doing. Watson was the spokesman for the ambushers.

"Blake," he said, "you've had this coming for a long time. I've seen some rotten bastards in my time but you top them all. Anybody that would take advantage of a poor little blind girl ought to be killed instead of just being beaten up. But I'm telling you now, if I ever hear of you going over there again I'll personally kill you. Do you understand?"

"Yes, I understand. I understand your jealousy."

"No," he said. "I guess you wouldn't understand. That's why I'm telling you."

Ducky picked up a piece of wood and started for me. "Let me kill him now," he said.

"No," Watson said. "He isn't worth it." They went on toward the *barrio* and I limped back to the barracks.

For several days after that I was black and blue, and I had lost a tooth during the fracas. My one small satisfaction was the black eye I'd given to Ducky Halpert. It is best to avoid vicious people. I never went back to see Elena. I still believe Airman First Class Watson would have killed me if I had gone back, but now I shall never know.

Poor Elena Espeneida, my little lost brown flower. May this stupid world treat you kindly and may your days be short and sweet.

Third Entry (Undated)

I BELIEVE I should write something about the miserable quality of the food at this dark field. It is certainly most unreasonable to station a man in the midst of nowhere and then go off and leave him with a storeroom containing nothing except canned corned beef and small, white dried beans. The first week or two the rations were all right. I managed to eat the stuff three times a day, but now I can eat only one meal a day and I have to force myself to do that.

There is no variety. To be sure, there is the choice of one or the other, and for a short time I could spend a few moments in thought as to which it would be, or both. But now, the thought that I have to eat either one makes my stomach turn over with disgust. So what I do is just put a pot of beans on the stove and dump a can of corned beef into it. This horrible mess simmers along, and when it begins to dry out I throw more snow into it. This concoction I eat once a day. And that is one too many times.

Often at night I dream of meat, of the huge hamburgers I used to buy in the summertime at Ocean Park, with the thick slice of tomato, the slab of Bermuda onion, the relish, the mustard, the thinly sliced tart dill pickle, and the great quarter pound patty of meat; hot, greasy and dripping. The dream wakes me, and I find that I've been drooling in my sleep; and in the dead silent air of my sleeping room I can almost smell the lingering traces of cooking hamburger and onions. At such times I'm so hungry it is impossible to go back to sleep. In desperation I go to the bean pot and take one huge bite of beans. I have to spit it out, finding that I cannot swallow such food with my recent visions so fresh in my mind.

The only virtue corned beef has is that it is greasy. By being careful I can scrape enough white fat from a newly opened can to wash my face and hands. It's as good, if not better, than regular soap. It is nice that the canned corned beef is good for something.

About my second or third week here I thought there might be game of some sort about. A country as wild as this should have some kind of animal living in it. It is wild enough for any animal. In addition to my daily round of the field I took a few short trips away from the field looking for tracks. I never found any. I haven't seen a bird, or even an insect for that matter. Of course, I can't go too far away from the tower. It's too cold, and a man could freeze quickly too long away from warmth. But there is nothing here anyway. Any animal who would pick this section of Tibet for a residence would be stupid.

In a way it is funny. There is food enough here to last one man for fifty years, and yet I am hungry. Really hungry.

I am hungry all the time.

Fourth Entry (Undated)

TODAY I HAVE been thinking about The Man in the Black Robe.

I know positively that there is such a Man and I wonder, sometimes, if He will find me here in Tibet, or wherever it is that I am now. So far, I haven't even seen His shadow. I doubt if He will ever come here for me, but I know that He exists. But at the time I didn't believe it. Only old Sinkiewicz believed it and he was right and I, for once, was wrong. Of course, the ten-day drunk Sinkiewicz was on had something to do with it. I have often noticed that alcohol sharpens a man's perception and he sees things he would not otherwise see. I suppose that is the way it was with old Sinkiewicz.

It was after midnight when the Pollack woke me. I was sleeping soundly and I shrugged his shaking hand away several times before I actually awoke. There he was, Airman Sinkiewicz, a four-day stubble of beard on his face, tears in his marbled eyes; thin arms jerking up and down in the moonlight like a man with Dengue fever.

"What'd you say, Sinkiewicz?" I asked him.

"The Man in the Black Robe . . ." he mumbled through his clattering false teeth. "He's after me again!"

"Look, Pop," I said, irritated, "go on back to bed and get some sleep."

"I haven't been to bed in three days, Blake! If I go to sleep now, He'll get me for sure!" Juicy tears rolled down his wrinkled cheeks. There is something horrible about an old man crying, and old Sinkiewicz must have been forty-five years old if he was a day. I swung my feet to the floor, pulled on my khaki shorts and lit a cigarette.

"What do you want me to do about it?" I asked wearily. I couldn't go back to sleep and let the old man cry.

"I need me some sleep, Blake; I ain't slept in three days. If you'll only stand guard for me, just an hour, that's all I ask, so I can get me some sleep, I can fight Him off when I wake up."

"Fight who off?"

"The Man in the Black Robe!" he whispered impatiently. "Who'd you think I was talking about?" He rubbed his eyes with the back of his right hand, trying to look at me and over his shoulder at the same time.

"Where is He?" I was interested. "I'd like to get a look at Him."

"You don't believe me, do you?"

"Sure. But I'd like to see Him, that's all."

Compressing his lips over his loose plate, Sinkiewicz nodded and weaved toward the stairwell. I followed, barefooted, exhilarated by the novelty of having something unexpected to do. Downstairs, on the long front gallery, Sinkiewicz retrieved his grande of gin from its hiding place behind the squadron bulletin board. He had a rough time taking out the cork, took a long pull, wiped the neck on his shirt and handed the bottle to me. I took a short one, and returned the bottle.

"Thanks. Now where is The Man in the Black Robe?"

"Follow me." Sinkiewicz held his shoulders back; the drink had steadied him. Doing his best to stay on tip-toes, he staggered down the porch. I padded along behind and when we reached the end of the barracks I came to an abrupt halt when he flattened his back to the wall and pointed a trembling finger around the corner of the building.

"The Man in the Black Robe!" he whispered dramatically.

Cautiously, I peeked around the corner and took in the scene. There was a pile of wood, ready for the kitchen stove in the morning; three windblown bamboo trees; the woodshed; and the well-known row of tightly covered garbage cans. Nothing else that I could see.

"Do you see Him?" Sinkiewicz hissed anxiously.

"No."

"Let me look!" Gripping my arms at the biceps, he peered over my shoulder. Quickly pulling his head back, he flattened his back to the wall again and trembled all over like a twanged rubber band. "He's there all right! Waiting for me behind the bamboo tree!"

I looked again. All I could see by the bamboo cluster were the wavering shadows caused by the slight breeze wafting up from the south. The moon was three-quarter and if there had been anything else back there I would have been able to see it with ease. My vision is fifteen-fifteen.

"You're nuts," I said. "There's nobody back there."

"You don't believe me," Sinkiewicz said childishly. A moment later, tears rolled down his cheeks again.

"Quit crying, for Christ's sake. Go on up to your bunk

and I'll stay down here on guard for you." I was trying to humor him, but he shook his head craftily.

"Best not to go inside. Too dark. I'll just lay the body down right here and you watch me for one hour. Okay? One hour. That's all I ask."

"All right."

I don't suppose the old rummy had slept for three days at that. As soon as he stretched his skinny body out on the porch he began to snore. Taking another shot of gin from his bottle I returned to my bunk. I took the gin along with me and stowed it away in my footlocker before climbing back into bed. Sinkiewicz had been drunk too long; it was time for him to taper off. Without further thought about the matter, I fell asleep and didn't wake until first call.

The Charge-of-Quarters found Sinkiewicz at 9:30 A.M. the next morning. His head was bashed in at the back and he was curled up fetuslike on the concrete floor of the shower boiler room. I happened to be in the barracks when the C.Q. found him because I had just returned from sick call. The C.Q., Staff Sergeant Haxby, was all excited by his find and I followed the crowd into the boiler room. Haxby, the mess sergeant, the first sergeant, two Filipino K.P.'s, Sinkiewicz and myself, made quite a crowd in the little room. A few other men, off-duty, hovered about outside the door. A good ten feet above the floor, on the concrete wall, there was a bloody spot as big as a man's hand. A few brown hairs, the same color as Sinkiewicz's hair, were mixed with the blood. A mystery. But a mystery easily solved by the brainy first sergeant.

"Here's the way I construct it," the Top said, pursing his lips. "Old Sinkiewicz was hanging by his knees from that pipe up there, and by swinging himself back and forth he kept banging his head against the wall until he killed himself."

"That must've been the way it happened, Top," Sergeant Haxby agreed.

"I don't think so," I said.

"Who asked you, Blake?" The first sergeant turned on me angrily. "And how come you ain't down on the line anyway?"

"I just got back from sick call."

"Then get your ass down to the line! You think I don't know a suicide when I see one?"

"Clear-cut," I said, and I left the boiler room, thereby making room for another observer.

The ambulance pulled up quietly as I started down the dirt road toward the hangar. The correct thing to have done, I suppose, would have been for me to tell the doctor about The Man in the Black Robe, but if I had, all I would have received for my pains would have been a reputation for being nuts. I ended up by not telling anybody anything about The Man in the Black Robe, and I suppose it is just as well. But now that it is written down; even on paper it doesn't make a hell of a lot of difference.

Not to me, anyway.

And I'll never see The Man in the Black Robe in this lousy place.

Fifth Entry (Undated)

TONIGHT I AM really excited and it is with great pride that I make this entry in my journal. Many days have passed by and I have entered nothing. I have entered nothing because nothing happens here. And to describe things of no consequence doesn't seem to be quite right. But all day today I've been writing a poem. In fact, I was so engrossed in it I almost forgot to make the rounds of the field to check the little red and green lights. But I did remember, and now; as the night hangs over the dark field like the evil witch she is; and as my search-

light shows her up every sixty seconds, I can inscribe
the poem I have labored on all day. It is beautiful and
true and sad and it almost has the answer . . . I wonder
why I didn't know before this that the fashioning of a
poem could bring such bittersweet tragedy to a young
man's heart?

MY HOUSE

My house has windows and doors that open both ways.
My house catches the night's southern rays.
The silence of death sleeps in my house.
And I am alone, all alone in my house.
My calling calls for the light of blackness
With a single searching ray of infrared—
Turning inward to see inside my shaking head.
This is my house, a vessel for my clumsy soul,
Set aside to repeat a senseless role,
Again and again throughout the matchless blackness.
Come Witch! And come Ghoul!
Let us examine the stool.
Let us see the beginning of that which is not
Outside the center of this house's inner rot!
For I am the Kingdom and the Glory for all Time;
The unheard lyrics of a speechless mime.

                                        And
My house has windows and doors that open both ways.
                                        And
My house catches the night's southern rays.

This is a very sad poem. And what makes it sadder
still is that I cannot share it with anybody. I've never been
one to talk much. I have been, if anything, a man of
action. It is boring to talk to strangers and fools and
most people are one or the other. But I have always liked
to listen to people talking, and now, even that is denied
me. I listen instead to the two-cylinder engine and the
generator. I listen to the wind as it whips out of the

western pass. I listen to the softly falling snow, and it is like listening to nothing. There is an air of futile unreality about this dark field that bothers me. I feel, sometimes, that I have been forgotten here, that I have been left here on purpose and that they don't intend to replace me . . . that I have been left here forever. Yet I know that such a thing is impossible. Every Air Force man must be accounted for, someplace. Although I am only a Basic Airman, I have my own little square in a column headed AMN on a morning report somewhere, and I cannot mean nothing. There has been some oversight. They are having difficulty in finding a replacement. That may be the answer. Perhaps the weather for flying is too bad? Many things can go wrong. But forgotten? It makes me laugh. No. I am not forgotten. Not me. Not Jacob C. Blake. I am a poet.

A poet cannot be forgotten.

Sixth Entry (Undated)

LAST NIGHT I couldn't sleep. I am never tired, but usually I can get to sleep all right; last night I couldn't. Without cigarettes, without coffee, without anything to read I was restless. It was too cold to go outside, so I decided to tire myself by doing calisthenics.

I ran through all of the exercises I could remember from basic training at Lackland Air Force Base, and then finished by doing pushups. Pushups are hard, and I had never been able to do more than twenty-five in my entire life. But last night I started, and I counted as I did each one, counting aloud, and I passed twenty-five, kept going, hit fifty, and when I got to one hundred I stopped of my own accord and sat down on the edge of my bunk.

One hundred! And I wasn't a bit tired; I could have kept on doing pushups all night long, two hundred, a thousand of them if I wanted. Just before making this entry I did a hundred pushups and I wasn't even breathing hard.

So one thing I can say for the dark field. It is healthy. Despite the lousy chow and all I am in better physical shape now than I have ever been in my entire life. I'm going to do some more.

I did five hundred. Nothing to it.

Seventh Entry (Undated)

IT WAS SUNDAY MORNING. I was in bed and Red Galvin was shaking me by the shoulder. It was Flagellante Day and I had forgotten.

"Get up," he said. "It's after seven." Galvin was dressed and when he saw that I was awake he left me and went downstairs. I put on a pair of khaki shorts and a polo shirt and joined Galvin in the dayroom.

"We can eat breakfast at the Iron Star in Angeles," he said. "Did you ever eat coconut pancakes dripping with rancid goat butter?"

"No." I shook my head sleepily.

"A fine way to start the day."

The taxi arrived and we rode to Angeles in silence. I was far from enthusiastic about seeing the Flagellantes but Red had been insistent that I go with him.

"These guys are true religious fanatics," he said. "A man should always observe fanaticism when he gets the chance. It is rare when people can be anything about anything, and maybe we can learn something."

"What can you learn from a bunch of Filipinos beating themselves with bamboo whips?" I asked.

"Love," Galvin said, and he would have spat out the window but it wasn't rolled down.

The taxicab pulled up and stopped in front of the Iron Star and I signed the chit.

We ate breakfast at the Iron Star and the pancakes

were all right. The goat butter wasn't. I'm not much for
goat butter. Several whores from the Bull-Pen, hearing
that two airmen were in town already, began to drift
sleepily into the Iron Star. The Moro, two Elena's, The
Igorote and Blondie were among the first arrivals. I didn't
like to look at Blondie. She had peroxided her hair with
terrible success, and it was an ugly reddish-orange color
with the jet roots growing out again for almost an inch
close to her dirty scalp. Despite the weird color of her
hair she got a surprising play on payday.

Red sent the Moro to the Chinaman's for a bottle of
gin. We sat drinking gin highballs until ten-thirty. It was
hot by that time and I was feeling the effects of the gin. It
was pleasant, sitting there, looking across the dusty plaza
at the dancing heatwaves.

"It should be about time," Red said. We left the semi-
coolness of the Iron Star and started out for the white-
washed church and the beginning of the climb. Before we
reached the church we got another grande of gin at the
Chinaman's. A Filipino and his young girl friend were in
the Chinaman's and Galvin patted the girl on her rear
end. Her boy friend didn't like it and shoved Galvin. Galvin hit the man in the stomach and he doubled over, fell
on the floor, and was sick. The girl ran into the back
darkened section of the store and, trembling, flattened
herself against the wall.

"Never push a redhead," Galvin told the man on the
floor. I signed a chit for the grande and we went to the
church.

There was a large crowd gathered. Several officers
and their dependents were in the crowd, all of them with
cameras, taking pictures of the Flagellantes. A couple of
dependents gave Galvin and me dirty looks, but the officers pretended not to notice us. The Flagellantes were
getting into the mood; about twenty-five of them altogether. Fiber ropes were tied tightly around their arms
and legs and more than half of them wore heavy crosses

tied across their backs. They held limp bamboo switches in each hand which they swished gingerly across their backs as the priest chanted to them. There was a huge crowd of Filipinos, all of them dressed in their best clothes. The women prayed and counted the number of beads on their rosaries. It was a colorful sight and I was glad I was there to see it.

The procession started, the black-robed priest leading the way. The Flagellantes were going to end up at a hilltop almost three miles away for the finish of the ceremony. They seemed to get more fervor as the climb started and were soon switching themselves very hard. Their backs began to bleed and from time to time they would shout in ecstasy; bitter, incomprehensible cries.

Galvin and I followed along, stopping now and then to have a drink from the bottle. The crowd thinned quickly, officers and dependents being the first to leave. It was really too hot to be out in the blazing sun. Perspiration ran down my bare legs and squished in my shoes as I walked. We had started with the head of the column, but after stopping a few times we were all alone on the trail.

"The hell with this," I said. "Let's sit down."

"I guess we've seen enough for one day at that," Galvin said.

We sat on a cluster of rocks by the side of the trail under the shade of a banana tree. I took a long swig of gin. The searing fluid burned my throat and filled me with elation.

"Yaow!" I yelled.

Galvin had another drink but he didn't yell. He was more dignified with every drink. The last of the Flagellantes was coming up the hill. I nudged Galvin and we watched the man struggle up the steep incline. He was small, even for a Filipino, and his cross appeared to be much larger and heavier than those of the other Flagellantes. His dark, sienna body was drenched with sweat and his arms were streaked with blood from cross-handed switching with the sharp twisted strips of bamboo.

As he came abreast of us he dropped, exhausted, to the ground. He struggled to rise, couldn't and then lay there in the dust, shuddering with great rasping sobs. It made me more tired than I was already just to listen to him.

Galvin got up from his rock and kicked the Flagellante in the ribs. I heard the ribs crack, and I could see the scuffed skin on the man's side where the point of Galvin's heavy shoe had landed.

"Get up," Galvin said, and he kicked him again. The man made no effort to rise. Galvin kicked him in the face and blood ran from the man's mouth, bubbling. I watched his eyes. They were the eyes of a dog with a full belly; full to bursting, and yet begging at the table for more food. He didn't cry out. There wasn't a shred of hate in his eyes. Just love.

"You wanted to suffer. Now suffer!" Galvin said, and he kicked him in the head again. The man continued his rasping breathing. Galvin sat down and we had another drink.

"Galvin," I said, "this man loves us." It was hard to believe but I knew it was so. I could see it in the man's eyes. The realization was like an electric shock to me.

"Sure he does," Galvin said. "Today he is Jesus. But watch out for the sonofabitch tomorrow. He'll cut your head off with a *bolo*."

"No. Not this man. He loves us." I began to cry. I couldn't help it. "No one has ever loved me before," I said.

"You're drunk, you bastard," Galvin said.

This was true. I was very drunk. Yet I knew this little Flagellante loved me and it made me cry. Sobbing, I got to my feet. I wanted to help the Flagellante up, but I tripped over the cross and fell down. This made Galvin laugh and in a moment I was laughing too. We killed the remainder of the gin, and leaving the man in the middle of the trail, we lurched down the hill.

We were singing when we reached Angeles again. We had a drink at the Chinaman's and I signed a chit for another grande of gin. The young girl came into the store, the same girl Glavin had patted before we left. She saw Galvin and tried to run out, but he caught her by the arm and held her.

"I'm going to the Iron Star," I said.

"Go ahead." Galvin didn't look at me. He was holding the girl with one hand and tickling her with the other. She squirmed and kicked him. The Chinaman was giggling like he was the one being tickled.

Sergeant Ratilinsky was sitting at a table in the Iron Star eating a big bowlful of *pansit*. He waved me over and I ordered a bowl for myself. After we ate, we drank gin highballs made with *lemonada*. A Filipino Army recruit came into the cafe wearing a .45 pistol on his hip.

"Do you know how to take that gun apart, boy?" Sergeant Ratilinsky asked him.

"No, sir." He handed his weapon obediently to Ratilinsky, when the sergeant held out his hand.

Ratilinsky detail-stripped the pistol down as far as it would go. The parts were spread all over the top of the greasy, *pansit*-smeared table. I was laughing. Ratilinsky had a false look of intense concentration on his face. He eyed the scattered pistol stupidly. He scratched his head.

"Do you know how to put this gun together again, boy?" he asked the young soldier.

"No, sir."

"Neither do I," Sergeant Ratilinsky said, with a straight face.

I was laughing so hard by that time I fell off my chair. No sounds were coming from my throat. It was a terrible breath-choking laugh. The old *mamasan* came from behind the counter and stood over me.

"Whassa matter, you? Whassa matter, you?" she asked.

I passed out.

Later I remember riding back to the field in a taxi with Abe Harris and Sergeant Ratilinsky. Abe spotted Galvin lying by the side of the road and we had the driver stop. He was dead weight and we had to drag him into the taxi.

At the barracks I was sobered quite a bit from the ride, and I helped Abe carry Galvin upstairs. We threw him on his bunk.

The next morning Red Galvin was dead. Somebody had stabbed him with a knife. It must have been a thin blade. He bled internally. Just to look at the tiny wound, it was nothing. The Air Police never found out who killed him.

The Sunday following his death, I picked some flowers in the jungle, walked to the base cemetery, and put them on his grave.

They were the only flowers he got.

Eighth Entry (Undated)

A STRANGE THING happened today and it adds to the evil that hangs over this dark field like a foul mildewed blanket.

I wanted to see what my beard looked like. Before coming here I shaved every day except Sunday. But in my haste to get here I only had four blades in my shaving kit. These were used up long ago and, consequently, my beard has grown thick and long since I stopped shaving. I don't have a mirror and I wondered what I looked like with a beard. I came up here to the tower and tried to catch my reflection in the window. I could not. I thought then that it was because I was on the inside lookout and the light wasn't right. I went outside and shifted a few empty fuel drums to make a sort of a ladder, and stood at the apex to look in the window from the outside.

I still couldn't see any reflection. All I could see was the inside of the tower room. It was disconcerting. I boiled a cup of water and drank it to settle my tense nerves. I still can't understand it.

I talked to myself about it. These conversations I hold with myself are more frequent of late, but they are harmless, and at times, interesting. I've divided myself into two persons to tell myself apart. The man with the beard is Mr. Blake and the man I was before without the beard is Jake. It's easier that way.

"Well, Jake," I said, "how do I look with a beard?"

"It does nothing for you."

"You'd say that, not having a beard yourself."

"Look for yourself then."

"I tried to and couldn't."

"Mr. Blake, I'm going to tell you something for your own good—"

"Don't tell me anything for my own good!" I broke in.

"All right. For my own good then. Having known you for a long time I feel I can speak frankly and sincerely to you. I've always had your welfare at heart even though I haven't always shown it by my actions."

"I know that, Jake. You're my best friend."

"I'm more than that. I'm your only friend."

"And that goes for me too."

"I'm filled with mutual admiration for you."

"With and without the beard?"

"With and without the beard."

"What were you going to tell me for my own good, Jake?"

"You can't see your reflection because you only see the things there are for you and not the things there are."

"Do you mind running over that again?"

"Not at all. Have you ever cast reflections on yourself?"

"Well, I . . ."

"Of course you haven't. It takes a person like myself, a man who is close to you, a friend, a confidant, to see and tell you of your imperfections."

"What makes you such an authority?" I scratched my throat through my beard.

"I can only reply with another question. Who knows you better than I know you?"

"That isn't an answer, Jake. When a man is standing too close, things become magnified in his eyes. He should stand back, way back, and get an overall picture."

"True. But if he gets too far away the imperfections have a tendency to diminish in his eyes."

"What's wrong with that?" I said innocently.

"Mr. Blake, Mr. Blake." I shook my head sadly. "You're hedging."

I shifted uncomfortably in my chair. The beardless youth was getting on my nerves.

"Now look here, Jake. You've got a bunch of generalizations stored up in that young mind of yours and none of them make any sense! If you're going to tell me something, tell it!"

"If you'll stop that scratching and listen for a minute I will tell you."

"The beard makes my neck itch. All right. I'll stop."

"Mr. Blake," I continued. "I've been doing a lot of thinking in the months I've been stationed here. In a way, this lonely assignment has been the best thing that ever happened to me. It's an opportunity few men get in a dreary lifetime. So involved are men with their foolish, but necessary, grubby, day to day existence, scratching around in the filth for wherewithal and sustenance; they never get the chance that you and I have: The chance to actually sit, to get completely rested, and to ask themselves, 'What is it all about?' and to then provide themselves with the answer. Do you follow me?"

"I'm listening. Go ahead."

"I've already said it. Ask yourself."

"You mean I should ask myself what it's all about?"

"Of course. Weren't you listening?"

"All right! What is it all about?" I asked it bitterly, and I didn't expect an answer.

"Open the door and look outside."

I opened the door. The sun was gone. It had gone down behind the western peak. It was dark; time to make my square of the field and check the lights.

I flicked the switches on, shrugged into the dirty sheepskin jacket, and by the light of the searchlight as it circled every sixty seconds, I made my rounds.

I still don't know what I look like with my beard, but I imagine I look as well as anyone else with one.

Ninth Entry (Undated)

I HAVE NOTICED, by keeping this journal, that I usually feel a lot better after writing something down. And it always gives me a lot of pleasure to go back over what I've written and read it. I only wish I was able to write something down every day. But I cannot. It is difficult to get started. It is hard to think of a subject, or a plan, and things are always more interesting when they are put down in a certain groove and lead up to something. My life so far has been so uneventful I must wrack my brain to think of anything worth writing and then I discard the ideas I do get as too mundane.

Tonight, though, I thought I would write about the Baluga. It could get me into trouble to write about it, should anybody get their hands on this journal, but I have never been sure I did the right thing in killing that Baluga anyway, and perhaps, by putting it down on paper, I might come to some sort of conclusion.

The Balugas of Pinatuba in the Philippines are a Negrito race; a race of little men and women rarely growing more than three and a half feet tall. They are mighty primitive, not even speaking Tagalog, the main Filipino dialect, and no English at all. Most of them live on and around Mount Pinatuba, eking out a bare existence by planting sweet potatoes, and by eating small animals they manage to bag with bows and arrows. They never wash and their little black bodies are scaly most of the time, unless they happen to be surprised by a quick tropical rain. Nearby our Pampanga field there was a small villageful of them, perhaps twenty families in all, and they were a bit more civilized than the rest of the tribe that lived on Mount Pinatuba. We airmen always passed through the little village on our way to the *barrio* and the Air Force Settlement. It was interesting to watch their activities in community living. There was one huge black pot in the middle of the sandy street, and the older Balugas, men and women, kept a hot fire going under it all of the time. The younger men, after foraging in the jungle, would throw what they caught or bagged into the pot. The young women would throw in sweet potatoes from time to time, or else wrap the potatoes in banana leaves and shove them under the coals. When hungry, they would pick up a pointed stick and stab it into the pot and eat what they speared; a lizard, a section of a snake, a field mouse, a portion of rabbit or a sweet potato. It was an honest, communistic way of living.

On paydays, five or six of the young Baluga men would come to the field and stand around hoping some airman would buy a bow and arrow set. In this manner the Balugas obtained cash. The arrows, as I recall, were three pesos apiece and the bows sold for ten. You couldn't haggle about price because they couldn't understand you. The price never varied and they wouldn't take five pesos for an arrow or two and a half; it had to be three. Several airmen bought sets consisting of a bow and three arrows and mailed them back to the States. I guess they wanted them for souvenirs. I never bought any because they were too crudely made to suit me, and besides, I wouldn't have had any use for them.

One of the Balugas worked for the squadron. He was very old, but his job wasn't difficult. He pulled a weighted burlap sack over the sand greens of our nine-hole golf course every day. It was a strange sight, when I first arrived at the field, to sit on the porch railing and look across the road to hole number five and see this tiny black man in a dirty loin cloth, clutching a bow and arrow in one hand and dragging a burlap sack around and around the sand green. He was serious about this work and I often wondered how the job had been explained to him in the first place. He didn't speak a word of English. On payday the Charge of Quarters would get a ten-peso check from the first sergeant and take the Baluga into the PX to cash it. The Baluga would make an X on the back, and after the CQ countersigned the check he would give the Baluga ten one-peso bills.

Many of the men tried to kid the old Baluga. They would question him and he always listened attentively. After listening for a decent interval he would say: *"Junque cigarillo mo!"* meaning, "Give me your cigarette!" or actually, to give him a cigarette. He would take the cigarette that was offered, light it, and put it between his teeth with the fire part inside his mouth and smoke it. The interview was over, so far as he was concerned, after he got the cigarette. He would leave then, and wouldn't be seen until the next day. There he would be again, out on the golf course dragging the burlap sack around the greens. After a few weeks I was used to the sight and it no longer seemed strange to me. I still can't work up any excitement about his death and it means nothing to me. Perhaps it should. That's why I'm writing this down; to see if I should be affected in any way with what happened. I would like to know.

Guard duty was a fairly simple matter at Pampanga. There were two posts, watchman type, the detail calling for two NCO's and four airmen. One post was at the hangar area and the other was around the barracks area and the officer's row. The shifts were from six to midnight and from midnight to six. The next day, following a guard shift, was an off day unless there happened to be a prisoner in our little guardhouse, and if there were, (sometimes Leech Hudson was in for a few days) the four Airmen of the guard split the day four ways and worked the prisoner. Guard duty wasn't too bad and it only came around about twice a month.

The night this happened I was on the midnight to six shift on Post Number Two; the barracks area and officer's row. There was a telephone in the dayroom by the barracks and another one in the garage at the end of the officer's row of houses behind a captain's residence. It took fifteen minutes to patrol from the dayroom to the garage and one of the orders was to call the sergeant of the guard every twenty minutes to tell him everything was all right. Once from the dayroom phone and twenty minutes later from the garage phone. I learned early in the game that it was just as easy to sit on a box in the garage and make several calls from there instead of doing the tedious patrolling and the sergeant wouldn't know the difference anyway. Another order on Post Number Two was to shoot all loose dogs. The reason for this order was that in the tropical heat the dogs that abounded in the *barrios* caught rabies quite easily, and the diet they lived on, consisting mostly of fish heads and the leftover rice the Filipinos gave them, caused them to lose their hair and raised large red sores on their bodies. Such an animal could spread disease. It was best to shoot them. I mention this order to prove I was entirely within my rights on this night I am writing about. The sentinel carried a riot gun, commonly called a sawed-off shotgun, and four shells. I was always on the lookout for dogs in the hope I could shoot one to break the monotony of the long night.

It was about 2 A.M. and I had just made a call from the garage telling the sergeant everything was okay. I saw a light coming down the alley and got to my feet, cocked my gun and took the safety off. I stepped out of the shadow and challenged.

"Halt! Who's there?"

The light kept coming. It was the old Baluga who worked on the golf course and he was carrying a candle stuck on a board. He stopped and grimaced at me, holding the candle up so I could see his face. He had no business being there at that time of night, but was using the alley as a shortcut to get to the trail leading to the Baluga village.

"Looks to me like you're lost, old man," I said.

"Junque cigarillo mo!" he said.

The feeling I got when he said those three words filled me with compassion for the old man. He was on the bottom rung of the ladder. It was a feeling of great pity I felt, and at the same time one of great love. It swelled inside me. I couldn't hold all of it. My heart was filled with the strong emotions. I wanted to do something for him. This primitive little man. He had nothing. He would never have anything.

I knew there was only one thing I could do for him and I had to do it. My eyes began to blur and just before the tears rolled down my cheeks I pulled the trigger. The shot caught him full in the chest and he fell backward, slammed to the ground. His candle went out as it fell in the thick dust of the alley. I put the safety on and stood silently for a full minute, listening to the night. It was a still night and I knew the sergeant of the guard heard the shot at the other end of the field. I called the guardhouse from the garage.

"This is Post Number Two, Sergeant Irby. I just shot at a dog, but I missed him."

"All right. I heard the shot. Be sure you get him next time. These shells cost the government twenty cents apiece."

"I know what they cost. I'm going to stay on the officer's row for a few more minutes in case he comes back."

"Okay," he said and he hung up.

That gave me twenty minutes before I had to call again. The tears that had been rolling down my cheeks were gone. My hands began to shake and I was afraid. I was afraid of being caught. Although my motives had been good and I had meant well, I knew that I would be court-martialed if they found me with a dead Baluga. I put the shotgun inside the garage by the telephone. I carried the dead Baluga into the open field behind the row of houses. It was a rocky field, scattered here and there with grey fieldstones and thick patches of lush grass. The Baluga was very light in my arms. I found a shallow sandy depression in the uneven field, scooped it deeper with my foot, and put the little man into it. I covered him with a layer of sand and small rocks and brushed the grave clear of footprints and markings with a piece of brush. I returned to the road for his bow and arrows and piece of board with candle. I buried these in the field. Looking at my watch I noticed the twenty minutes were up. I called the guardhouse.

"Post Number Two. Everything okay," I said.

"Did you see the dog again?"

"No. But I'm keeping an eye out."

"Okay." He hung up.

I knew I had to kill a dog; I had to kill one to dis-courage suspicion. Our squadron commander had a dog. Prince. A boxer. I took my shotgun and walked up the alley to the major's house. Prince was tied to his latticed doghouse in the back yard. He was awake and licked my hand when I patted him on the head. I untied him, and holding him by the collar, I led him down the alley for a hundred yards or so. Foolishly, I turned him loose and the frisky animal galloped away. He was playful and ran around in circles. He would jump up on me and then dart away. I called him softly. He paid no attention. I chased the beast and after five miserable minutes he allowed me to catch him. Holding him by the collar I held the muzzle of the shotgun against his side with my free hand and pulled the trigger. He dropped to the dust. I called the guardhouse.

"This is Post Number Two. I shot the dog."

"Good."

"I don't think it's a *barrio* dog though."

"You don't?"

"No. It looks a lot like Prince."

"The major's dog?"

"Yes. I think it is," I said.

"Jesus!"

"How was I to know? He was running loose."

"I'm coming up there. Wait for me by the garage phone."

Sergeant Irby examined Prince and we covered the dog with a burlap sack I found in the garage. He wrote a report for his guard book the way I described it. At 6 A.M. I was relieved. I ate breakfast in the mess hall and went to bed. I was dead tired.

At 10 A.M. the Charge of Quarters woke me.

"The major wants to see you in the orderly room. Get dressed."

"What does he want to see me about?" I asked.

"I can't imagine," the CQ said.

I reported to the first sergeant in the orderly room. I didn't like the first sergeant very well. He always had something unpleasant to say to everybody. He was in his late forties, bald, and his large teeth looked as if they were slipcovered with Muscat grape skins. His mouth was smiling at me.

"The old man wants to see you, Blake. Do you know how to report?"

"Of course I do."

"I suppose you've got a good story ready?"

"What do you mean, Sergeant?"

"All right, Blake. Report to the major."

I knocked on the inner door and the major told me to come in. I halted one pace away from his desk, saluted, and reported.

"Sir. Basic Airman Blake reports to the squadron commander as directed by the first sergeant."

He returned my salute and stared at me. His face was old; his skin was furrowed and creased with deep wrinkles. His eyes, however, were bright and alert. They looked me over like two tropical fish exploring a new aquarium.

"Blake. Why did you shoot my dog?"

"He was running loose. I didn't recognize him."

"You're a liar, Blake."

"No, sir."

"Then why did you shoot my dog?"

"He was running loose like I said, sir. I missed him with my first shot and then when he came around again I bagged him. I didn't know it was Prince, sir."

"Blake, there were powder burns on his side. The muzzle of that gun was so close the shot didn't even have a chance to scatter."

"He was running by me pretty fast, sir."

He didn't say anything for a long time. He just looked at me. I was still standing at attention. Perspiration was flowing down my back under my starched khaki shirt. I saw the tears start in his eyes, and I watched them roll down his cheeks. I was ashamed for him and then I was sorry for him. He felt about me just like I had felt about the Baluga. I was glad he didn't have a shotgun in his hand.

"That's all, Blake."

"Yes, sir." I saluted, did an about face, and closed the door behind me.

"You ought to feel real proud of yourself," the first sergeant said.

"I didn't write the guard orders. You people did," I said.

"Get the hell out of here!" he yelled at me. I went back to bed.

As far as I know they have never found the buried Baluga. I imagine the ants have got him by now.

Now that I've written all of this down I find that I still feel sorry for the Baluga. But unlike the major, at least I tried to do the right thing.

Tenth Entry (Undated)

I'VE STOPPED EATING altogether now. Just the last two days. I don't feel any ill effects at all. I feel much better in fact. I don't suppose I can continue to ignore food, but I've decided to try it for a while. I'm as strong as I ever was and can make my round of the field all right. After a few days I'll go back to eating one meal a day, but it's restful to know that I don't have to eat the horrible beans and corned beef for a few days.

If somebody were to come up to me now and say, "Blake, what do you want more than anything else in the world?" I would say, "Popcorn! And don't spare the butter!"

Eleventh Entry (Undated)

I STILL CAN'T understand why I was assigned to this field. I'm a truck driver not a maintenance man. It was probably the major's idea, because I'm certain he didn't like me after I shot his dog. But all the same, personal prejudice is not supposed to enter into the assignments of airmen, and perhaps it is wrong for me to blame the major for this assignment. He was just doing his duty, I imagine, and when my name came up for this job he gave it to me and let it go at that.

It was on a Saturday morning, right after the inspection. I was changing into khaki shorts and a polo shirt when the Charge of Quarters came running up the stairs screaming my name. Pollack NCO's always scream.

"I'm over here," I said. "I'm not deaf either."

"You've got to get hot, Blake," he said. "There's a plane waiting for you down on the line!" He was excited.

"A plane for what?"

"An 0-19. You're leaving."

"Leaving for where?"

"I don't know." He shrugged his shoulders. "The first sergeant called from the line and said for you to throw some stuff in a barracks bag. You're being transferred."

"What about my footlocker and my stuff in the laundry?"

"I don't know anything about that. I suppose it'll be sent to you. Here. I'll give you a hand." He threw my uniforms and stuff into a barracks bag while I changed back into my inspection uniform. I shouldered my barracks bag and went downstairs. The squadron jeep was out front and the driver drove me down to the flight line.

The major and the first sergeant were waiting for me by an all-fabric 0-19 that had its prop turning over. There was a pilot in the plane but I didn't know who he was. He had his helmet and goggles on and the lower part of his face was muffled by a white silk scarf. The major took me by the arm and led me away from the plane where it wasn't so noisy. The first sergeant threw my barracks bag into the rear cockpit.

"Blake," the major said, "you've been assigned to Tibet."

"Tibet?"

"Yes. You're assigned there temporarily as a field maintenance man. Your job is to keep the lights on at night, and act as alert man for any planes forced down in that area. You know how to service planes, don't you?"

"I drove the gas truck for two months."

"Fine."

"What about the rest of my stuff?"

"We'll send it to you. The pilot's waiting now, so you'd better hurry."

The first sergeant was holding a heavy flying suit for me and I struggled into it, putting it on over my uniform. I put on the helmet and the goggles he handed me and climbed into the plane. The pilot taxied to the end of the field. On the takeoff we passed in front of the hangar, and it looked like the entire squadron was in formation on the concrete apron, all of them at hand salute. It was nice of so many to see me off that way.

There wasn't any radio contact with the pilot from the rear cockpit. I looked around and couldn't find a headset. The pilot never turned around, but kept his eyes straight ahead, his mind on the business of flying the obsolete aircraft. After three hours we landed at a small grassy field and a Filipino boy gassed the ship. I started to dismount to help him but the pilot shook his head, no. We took off again.

We flew over water after that and were soon out of sight of land. The next stop was an island field. It was a little island and I didn't see it at first. There was a slight haze on the water and for a moment I thought the pilot was off his rocker, but then the bare, low-flying island appeared and he put the 0-19 down on a crushed coral strip. The man who gassed the plane this time had a turban wrapped around his head. I took him for a Hindu. We flew away from the island.

It began to get dark and it was cold. Despite the heavy flying suit the cold settled in my arms and back and I felt miserable. I didn't have flying boots on and my feet were like a couple of rocks. The night was black before the pilot set the plane down again. We landed on a small diamond-shaped field without landing lights; just the probing wing lights of the plane picking the way. We rolled to a stop and an ancient Chinaman hobbled out to the plane. Taxiing, the pilot followed the Chinaman to a stone shed and cut the engine. After we were refueled I yelled to the Chinaman.

"What have you got to eat?"

He didn't understand me. By sign language I got across the idea that I was hungry. He grinned, nodded his head, and brought me a can of corned beef from the stone shed. Before I got it open the pilot was taking off. I ate the corned beef in the plane. It was the last time I remember tasting corned beef and liking it.

There were two more similar stops for fuel before we started over the mountains. The pilot was a good one. I knew the ceiling was much too low for an old crate like the 0-19, yet he managed to nurse it up and up, the engine protesting every foot of ascent. He stayed in the passes as much as possible and at times I could see the snowy heights of mountains rising up and almost out of sight. Huge mountains they were, shaped like daggers, like bears, like dragons. I fell asleep after a time despite my growing numbness and when I awoke we were on the ground. The pilot was shaking me by the shoulder with his gloved hand. When he saw I was awake he pointed to the tower of this dark field and signaled for me to get out. I got out with my barracks bag, took off the flying suit and helmet and handed them up to him. The prop was still whirring and without a word he twisted the ship about, catching me with a blast of icy propwash. I dodged back as he taxied to the end of the field. I watched him take off and fly into the opening of the pass; then I lost sight of the plane as it disappeared into the gently falling snow. He could have waved goodbye to me. I expected it. But he didn't.

Shivering in my khakis I ran to the tower, threw my barracks bag on the floor and started the gas stove. I ate a can of corned beef. I found the gasoline engine, started it; found the light switches and turned them on. I've been here ever since. I have been ready to leave ever since that first night.

I am overdue for a change of assignment.
I must be.

Twelfth Entry (Undated)

IT HAS NOW BEEN ten days since I've eaten anything. I still make hot water out of snow and drink it but I haven't tasted either beans or corned beef. I should feel weak but I feel stronger than I've ever felt in my life. I'm in a better humor too. I spent all morning singing all of the old songs I could remember. "Flirtation Walk," "Isn't It Romantic?," "You're the Top," lots of them. It's funny how the words to these songs come back to a man. I don't even remember learning most of them. "Deep Purple" brings back a lot of wonderful memories. All puppy love stuff of course, and of a girl who wouldn't interest me now, but the singing of the song brought many memories back to me. They were great days, those L.A days. Los Angeles is a wonderful city to grow up in. There are so many fine things to do in L.A. Childhood, after everything is said and done, is perhaps the best time of all.

I didn't like school when I was growing up, but none of the guys did. It was so dull. I passed every time but so did everyone else. They have to pass you on to the next class. Other kids are pushing their way up and if they didn't pass you there wouldn't be any room. "Deep Purple" is a good song. Probably the best song ever written. I thought of a little prayer.

If I should die before I eat,
I pray the Lord my soul to meet.

It's a funny little poem, sardonic too, a twist on the regular bedtime prayer they teach to kids. *If I should die before I wake, I pray the Lord my soul to take.* Mine is

better. I'm not going to die anyway. I'll be right here
when the time comes to leave. There is a lot of back pay
coming to me and I intend to draw and spend every cent
of it. This afternoon, even if I have to force myself I'm
going to start eating again. I feel good today. Real good.

This dark field isn't so bad once you get used to it. At
first I couldn't see it. It was too lonely. But it's good to
be by yourself. It gives a man a chance to realize some
of the mistakes he has made. If I had it to do all over again
I wouldn't have enlisted in the service. I'd have gotten
married, gone to college, or maybe to a good trade school.
But it isn't too late to do any of these things. When my
enlistment is up I can still go to school. I can start all
over again. I'll be all the wiser for this experience. Certainly I will. I know one thing. They can't keep me at this
field after my enlistment is up. That's one thing they
can't do. It's the law. So why shouldn't I feel happy?

What I'm going to do right now is go downstairs and
cook up a big pot of beans and eat every bite. Then I'm
going to sing some more old songs. My baritone sounds
pretty good. If I practice singing every day and get so
I'm really good at it I can sing in night clubs when I get
out. Make records. Might get in the big money. I don't
smoke anymore. I don't even miss the cigarettes anymore.
That's why my voice sounds so good.

After looking this entry over I see it doesn't mean
much. But in case I don't feel so happy after a couple of
days I can come back and reread it.

At least I feel happy today!

Last Entry (Undated)

I MIGHT as well tie this up.

Two hours ago I was making my daily round of the
field. I was replacing a burned-out bulb in one of the field
lights almost directly across the field from the tower.
Then I heard my name.

"AIRMAN JAKE BLAKE! REPORT TO THE TOWER!"

I ran, running as fast as I've ever run in my life. All the way across the field my name kept booming out of the tower: "BLAKE! COME IN, BLAKE! BLAKE! COME IN, BLAKE!" I cursed myself as I ran for my attention to duty.

I reached the big oak door and pulled it open. The voice was booming from upstairs. I climbed the ladder. The voice was coming out of the speaker. The radio equipment on all three sides of the tower room was brilliantly lighted; humming like a million bees; the radio equipment that had never worked in all the time I'd been there! I searched frantically for the microphone, found it, plugged it into the female socket.

"Blake!" I yelled. "This is Blake! Come in!" I was out of breath.

"AIRMAN BLAKE?" the voice asked.

"Who else!" I shouted bitterly. I couldn't help it.

"GET READY TO LEAVE."

"When?"

"GET READY TO LEAVE. OVER AND OUT."

The transmitter and receiver lights went off. Click! The angry humming stopped. The room was silent again. More silent than ever. I stared dumbly at the speaker. Had I heard it speak? Did a voice tell me to get ready to leave or was everything a dream? I was still panting, puffing, out of breath. I knew that I'd heard the voice and yet I couldn't believe it. I felt the top of the transmitter. It was warm!

"Yaow!" I shouted.

Downstairs, I stuffed my uniforms and underwear into my barracks bag. I brought this ledger and the ballpoint pen I'm writing with from upstairs, threw them into the bag. I stripped off my dirty sheepskin jacket and tossed it on the bunk. There would be another man to take my place and he would need it. For a moment I almost felt sorry for my unknown replacement. But I was too elated to feel sorry for anyone very long. I climbed to the tower and watched the opening in the pass for the airplane that was to take me away.

I could hear the plane before I could see it. It was a two-engine job. The engines weren't synchronized and I could hear them counter-coughing at each other. The transport loomed in the pass like a silver angel, leveled, and roared down to a perfect landing. I dropped down the ladder, grabbed my barracks bag, opened the door, and rushed onto the field. The door opened as I reached the plane. There wasn't a ladder and there wasn't anybody to give me a hand up, but I didn't mind that. I threw my bag in, and pulled myself up and over the edge of the doorway. As I got to my feet inside the door slammed shut. The plane taxied to the end of the runway. With an accelerated roar it picked up flying speed down the field and in a moment was airborne and heading for the pass. I didn't look out the window at the dark field. I never wanted to see it again, and I still don't.

Except for myself, my barracks bag, and a parachute with my name stenciled on it, the interior of the massive ship was empty. The door leading to the pilot's compartment was closed and I wanted to talk to him. I wanted to talk to anybody. But I waited. The pilot would have to clear the pass and I didn't want to interfere with his flying.

After waiting for approximately five minutes I opened the door to the cockpit.

There wasn't any pilot.

There was no one in the pilot's compartment.

The controls were steady as I watched them. The instruments on the panel reflected the things that were happening. The altimeter, air speed, all of the instruments were working nicely, but there was no one in the airplane except myself.

There still isn't.

I sat down on the floor next to my barracks bag. I don't

know how long I sat without moving, but I know it was quite a while. I was in a state of semi-shock or something as the realization of my predicament overwhelmed me. The plane roared through the night. It sank in after a while as I stared at the parachute. I didn't have to stay in the airplane. I could slip into the parachute, so kindly provided, open the door, and jump. So easy. Well, I don't want the easy way.

I opened the door and kicked the parachute out. No, Jacob C. Blake is not so easily tricked. After being stationed at the dark field for as long as I have been, I'll just go ahead and take my chances on my next assignment.

Either place—so long as there are people—will suit me right down to the ground—

(The journal breaks off here.)

"JUST LIKE ON TELEVISION—"

Arresting Off.:
Det. Sgt. G.E. Rouse, LAPD

Interviewing Off.:
Det. Lt. E.M. Harbold, LAPD

STATEMENT

I.O.: State your name and address.
Suspect: Billy T. Berkowitz. 3428½ South Normandy. The half's because I live around to the back. It's a garage apartment, but I don't have a car or anything—
I.O.: Simply answer the questions. Where do you live?
Suspect: I just said: 3428½ South—
I.O.: No, no. The city.
Suspect: Jesus. Los Angeles. Where else?
I.O.: And your full name?
Suspect: Billy T. Berko—
I.O.: The "T"; what's the "T" stand for?
Suspect: That's okay, I never use my middle name.
I.O.: We don't give a damn whether you use it or not. What's your middle name?
Suspect: Terence. After my grandfather; he was Irish.
I.O.: Is that your real middle name? You don't look Irish to me.
Suspect: I never said I was Irish; I said my grandfather was Irish.
I.O.: — — —. Never mind that, Steno, strike it out. Now, Billy, tell us in your own words about your move-

ments on October 23. Start in the morning, and finish up with the morning of the twenty-fourth. Do you understand? And remember that although this statement is voluntary, it may be used against you.

Suspect: I got to go back further than that. I can't explain everything right if I have to start on the morning of the twenty-third, because I just went to work like always.

I.O.:   All right. How far back?

Suspect: Not far. Just enough to explain my original idea, because it's a little involved. But it didn't come to me all at once, so it stands to reason I can't explain it all at once, don't it?

I.O.:   Go ahead.

Suspect: Television. That's where I got the idea. I watch TV every night, but I don't have no set of my own so I look at the sets in the four different bars I hang around in regular. That's what I am; I'm what you might call a habitué, a cocktail bar habitué—although I'm a beer drinker, not a hard liquor man. Not that I wouldn't drink whiskey all the time if I could afford it, but with my lousy job at only forty-five bucks a week and all—

I.O.:   Get on with it, Billy.

Suspect: I am getting on with it, but this is the background part, and if you don't have the fill-in part, the rest don't make sense. It was funny the way the idea came to me—not laughing funny, but funny funny, the way this idea came to me. Just like that. And from television, too.

Now my favorite kind of TV show is the private eye type—*Sunset Strip, Boston Blackie* reruns, *Mike Hammer, Hawaiian Eye*—

I.O.:   Skip the commercials.

Suspect: I'm only trying to explain the kind of shows I like. Anyway, I guess there are two or three good private eye shows every night, and knowing the schedule so well,

I don't miss many. Even when I was going from one bar to the next on my regular rounds I'd plan my time so I wouldn't miss a private eye show. It was research to watch them, to improve my business. In fact, if you will take a look in my little notebook you took away from me you'll see the way I've got them all rated. I give four stars for "superior," three stars for "excellent," two—

I.O.: We aren't interested in your TV ratings.

Suspect: Well, no, I guess not. My ratings don't mean much, except to me, but a man has got to set up some sort of a standard to go by. And watching all these private eye shows, especially the series kind, nursing a beer—making only forty-five bucks a week at the supermarket, I have to nurse one beer a long time, except when somebody buys me a free one, but I don't like to accept a free one because they expect you to buy one back, and—

I.O.: Get to the point, if there is a point.

Suspect: Sure there's a point. The point is this: By concentrating on this one kind of show, just because I liked them at first, after a while I began to see the pattern—the formula, you might call it. I don't mean all private eye shows are alike, I mean exactly the same, the way Westerns are; I mean that all these detectives, the private eyes, have a regular routine they more or less have to follow to solve the case. And it stands to reason that when most of these shows are a half-hour long, and the hero has to find the guy he's looking for to solve the case in a hurry, he has got a tough problem. So what does he do?

Just like in real life, the way any detective works—when he has to find out where somebody lives he has to ask some guy who knows. Like here in L.A., where most of the private eye shows take place. If you're hunting for some guy, what do you do—? Start down the street in any old direction knocking on every single door asking for the guy? Of course not. You'd never find him that way, and especially you wouldn't in a half-hour TV show. So in every show, they all got this one thing in common, there's always one guy who knows the answer. It had to be that way, I figured, and they just don't make up people like that for TV, either. The way I saw it there had to be a few guys in every town a cop or a private eye could go to and find out where the guy he was looking for lived. Or where he happened to be at that particular time.

I.O.: You're a thinker, Billy, a real thinker.

Suspect: Thanks. And that was my original idea, you see, that's the idea that came to me. After all, I thought, what did I do after work anyway? I work six days—Saturday's our biggest day at the supermarket—but when I get through, there are only two choices of something to do. I can go home to my cruddy garage apartment where there isn't anything to do, or I can go to a bar somewhere, nurse a beer, and watch TV. I could go to the movies, I suppose, but TV doesn't cost anything, and it is about the same anyway except for the smaller screen.

So when I got this idea I really got excited.

I.O.: What idea?

Suspect: The pattern. Becoming a part of the pattern. I realized that I could become a part of the detective work, the private eye pattern myself. After work. I even had the right kind of qualifications, just like the actors who played this kind of part on TV. For one thing, the guy the private eye asks for information is always a character. That was me; I'm something of a character myself.

I.O.: You are a character all right.

Suspect: Thanks. And another thing. The guy who hangs around in the bar knowing where everybody is—well, it's not easy to come right out and admit it this way—he always has what you might call an "obnoxious personality." And for some reason—I don't know why—I seem to be a little obnoxious to other people. I try to be friendly and all, but most people just don't like me very much. But in this case, when I thought it over, having this somewhat obnoxious personality, and being something of a character besides, well, it made me a natural for the barroom habitué and answerman. Here was a way for me to make a little dough on the side. Once I got myself established in the pattern I knew I could make some extra money this way.

I.O.:   How?

Suspect: How? I'm coming to that. Let me give you an example. Take any regular private eye half-hour story. Here's one that is used every week or so.

Some criminal, usually an escaped criminal from prison, hates the private eye hero and wants to kill him. So what he does first, he kidnaps the private eye's girl friend. The hero goes out with his gun looking for the kidnaper. He knows his name because somebody telephones him, or else there's a note slipped under his door. But he don't know where the kidnaper's hideout is, and he has to find out quick. What the criminal-kidnaper usually does, you see, to add a little suspense to the story, is to have the girl friend call the eye. Then he pinches her or something to make her scream over the phone, and then he hangs up quick. This drives the eye crazy. So the angry hero drives his convertible to some particular bar where there's a habitué who always knows where everybody is all the time.

The detective orders a drink, and looks sideways at the habitué, who is usually a little drunk.

"You know Blackjack Mussurgorsky?" the hero asks the habitué—

I.O.:   Spell that out.

Suspect: I don't know how to spell it; I just made it up. I think he was a football player or something, I don't know.

I.O.:   Okay. Go on.

Suspect: Anyway, the habitué just sits there; he don't even look at the private eye. "The name is not unfamiliar," he says, real cool-like. "Blackjack Matthews—"

I.O.: You said Mussurgorsky before.

Suspect: But now I'm giving you the guy's real name, which could have been Matthews, the other name being an alias, or something. I'm trying to make this up as I go along, and when you break in this way I forget where I was—

I.O.: Go on. Get on with it.

Suspect: All right. So the habitué says, real cool, you know: "Blackjack Mussurgorsky—"

I.O.: Make up your mind. Mussurgorsky or Matthews? You're confusing the steno.

Steno: No, he isn't.

Suspect: Mussurgorsky. And then the habitué says, "Whittier Reformatory for Boys, 1933–36; Preston Industrial Reformatory for Youthful Offenders, 1939–41; San Quentin, 1947–51; and Folsom Prison, 1953–57. Occupation: Strongarm boy, armed robbery, and handy with a rod."

The private eye nods his head—

I.O.: Just a minute. Sergeant Rouse. Run a make on Blackjack Mussurgorsky.

Sgt. Rouse: Yes, sir. Matthews, too?

I.O.: Yes, Matthews, too.

Suspect: But I made those names up, I told you—

I.O.: Never mind. Get on with it.

Suspect: Where was I?

Steno: "The private eye nods his head—"

Suspect: Right. And he says, the private eye says, "That's Blackjack Mussurgorsky, all right. Know where he is now?"

But this time the habitué doesn't say anything. Instead, he smiles *knowingly* into his drink. The eye gets the message, and lays a twenty-dollar bill on the bar. But the habitué ignores this bill; he waits for the eye to put another one down before he picks up the dough. "Try," he says then, "3428½ South Normandy. It's a salmon-colored duplex, upstairs."

I.O.: Not a garage apartment?

Suspect: I just used my own address for convenience. Anyway, that's the end of the habitué's part in the show. Of course, to finish the story, when the hero gets to 3428½ Normandy, or whatever the address is, he shoots it out with Blackjack Mussurgorsky, saves his girl friend, and that's the end of the show.

I.O.: Somehow, the point of all this escapes me.

Suspect: But that was me; that's what I wanted to be —a professional habitué, in real life. Only I must admit that I didn't know how to go about getting established at first. Before I could sell any information I had to get hold of some first, which only stands to reason. And that was the hardest part of the plan. First, I bought myself a notebook. Then I picked out the four nicest bars in my neighborhood and worked out a regular route and time schedule so I could hit each bar at the same time each night. Before the week was out I knew every bartender by name, and they all knew me as Billy. When I left one bar to go to the next, for instance, I'd tell the bartender, "Anybody asks for me, I'm at the Dew Drop Inn." Then when I got to the Dew Drop, I'd phone back to the bar I just left and ask the bartender if he'd seen Billy around tonight. And then he'd tell me over the phone that Billy had just left to go to the Dew Drop Inn. It was a good system, you see. When I got a chance to work it into a conversation, I'd say to these different bartenders, "I don't know how I do it, but I probably know more people in this neighborhood than anybody else." All this was groundwork, I figured, for later on.

Starting out with my new notebook, I wasn't selective about the names I put in it, because I really didn't know anybody at first. I picked up various names from listening in on bar conversations, and I always introduced myself to the strangers in various bars so they'd give me their names in return. Every time I picked up a new name I'd go into the men's room and write it down in my notebook.

I.O.: You just picked up names indiscriminately?

Suspect: I had to start somewhere, but getting the addresses was harder, the hardest part of all. A guy who's drinking will tell you his name all right, most of the time, anyway, but if you ask for his address he gets a little suspicious. So to tell you the truth, I got most of the addresses out of the phone book. If you know the name, that's the easiest way, if the guy's got a phone. If he hasn't, the next best bet is the City Register.

I.O.: This is a weird way to kill time in a bar.

Suspect: I guess it does sound a little weird, but like I said, I didn't have nothing else to do, and I figured that my information would pay off sooner or later. Just like on television. If I could pick up a few dollars, simply by giving out some guy's address to a private eye or a cop, well—do you have any idea what an extra ten bucks or so means to a guy who's only making forty-five a week?

I.O.: Get on with your statement.

Suspect: I'm coming to it now. It was about ten-fifteen, and I was in the Dew Drop Inn, 1425 Vermont Avenue, my regular bar for that time slot, and I was watching TV. There was only one other guy in the bar, not counting the bartender, Eddie McSwain, Figueroa Hotel, Room 419.

I.O.: Who was the other man?

Suspect: Mr. Bert Plouden, sells hand-painted neckties to exclusive shops; lives with his mother at 2715 41st Place.

I.O.: Don't you have to check your notebook for these addresses?

Suspect: No, it would be unprofessional. During the day at the supermarket, when I was stacking cans or something, I'd open the notebook and read one page over and over till I memorized all the names I had in the book.

And then it happened, just like a dream, or a private eye show coming to life. This man comes into the bar, goes straight to the bartender and shows him a photograph. It was a regular eight-by-ten photo, and I recognized the old *Dragnet* pattern right away. On *Dragnet* it's almost a *rule* for Sergeant Friday to carry a photo around to show bartenders.

"You know this woman?" the man asks Eddie. "She ever come in here?"

Eddie takes a look and shakes his head. Meantime, I'm watching the man close. Sure enough, I spot the bulge under his armpit, so I know he's got a pistol in a shoulder holster.

"I'm sorry," Eddie tells him, "but I've never seen her in here."

The man starts to leave, and then Eddie stopped him —just the way I knew he would when the right time came. "Hey!" Eddie says, "why don't you ask Billy?" He jerks his thumb at me. "Billy doesn't know how he does it, but he knows more people around here than anybody." Eddie was a little sarcastic, the way he said this, but I didn't mind. I wanted a look at the photograph. So the man comes down to my end of the bar and flashes the photo at me.

"D'you know this woman?"

Well, it just so happened that I did. Her name was Gloria, Gloria Latham. In fact, her name and address is the last entry listed in my little notebook. The whole thing was just a lucky accident, you might say. Only you can't really call it an accident, because I was in the *business* of getting names and addresses.

I'd met Miss Latham only the night before, just casually, in Skinny's Bar and Grill. Skinny's bar is always my last stop on the way home. Anyway, this Gloria Latham was pretty loaded. It was about fifteen minutes before closing, and she staggered when she went out the front door. She was too drunk to drive her car, and she knew it. I heard her tell the bartender, when he cautioned her about driving, that she was going to get a cab at the corner.

I.O.: Did you follow her outside?

Suspect: Sure, I followed her out. At this time, I only knew that her first name was Gloria. And I needed her last name to get her address out of the phone book. I was going to follow her to the cabstand and listen in if I could when she gave the hack driver her address. Then I could write it down, and check her last name later, you see. But there weren't any cabs at the stand. So I said to her, "Gloria, I'm Billy. I met you earlier at Skinny's tonight, if you remember—"

"Sure," she said, "I know you, Billy old Billy, old Billy goat you." Being intoxicated, she said my name that way three times—I don't know why, though.

"I don't have a car myself, Gloria," I told her, "but if you want me to take you home, I'll drive yours."

So even though she was really lit, she was smart enough to give me her car keys. And I drove her home —the Drexel Arms, 2746 Santa Barbara Avenue, Apartment 307. She gave me her address as soon as we got in the car, which was all I wanted. It was the only reason I offered to drive her home, but she didn't know that. I parked in front of the apartment house, helped her through the front door, and gave her back her keys.

I.O.: You didn't go into her apartment?

Suspect: No. By checking the row of mailboxes in the outside foyer I matched up Gloria to the last name— Latham—and wrote it down in my book, along with the address. The procedure was very simple; it was one of the easiest names and addresses I ever picked up.

I.O.: Then what did you do?

Suspect: I'm telling you now. I'm back in the bar now, as I said, looking at this photograph. And I see that it's Gloria Latham right away. But I play it cool. "Maybe I know her and maybe I don't," I say, and I shrug my shoulders.

He gives me the long look, the onceover, just like on TV, and then he frowns. "Take a better look," he says, real tough.

And I talked back just as tough. "I don't need another look." But I had a feeling that I wasn't getting through to the man, so I rubbed my thumb back and forth across my fingers. Everybody knows what that means; it's the signal to grease the old palm with cash. He gets the idea immediately, and puts a ten-dollar bill on the bar. I didn't try for a second tenner, the way they do on TV, I picked it up quick before he could change his mind.

"Her name is Gloria Latham."

"Do you know where she lives?"

I smile then, one of the knowing kinds, and then I figured that I might as well try for the second ten. So I make the old thumb and fingers rub again, and he puts down another ten-dollar bill. "The Drexel Arms," I told him, picking up the bill, "2746 Santa Barbara Avenue, Apartment 307."

"And your name is Billy?"

"That's right. Billy. Billy T. Berkowitz. And any time you need a little information, I'm right here in the Dew Drop every night from ten to eleven."

But when I reached back to get my wallet, in order to put the money away, he slapped the lousy handcuffs on me and brought me down here to the station. And I'm telling you again that I don't know anything else about the woman, just her name and address like I said. I certainly didn't kill her, for God's sake! I didn't even know she was dead till you guys told me she was. All I am is just a poor workingman with a lousy job in a supermarket. I was only trying to beat inflation by picking up a little extra dough as a professional barroom habitué. That's the whole truth, and I'll swear to it!

I.O.: Why did Miss Latham write "Billy" in lipstick on her bathroom mirror before she died?

Suspect: I don't know, but that don't mean I killed her! Being so drunk and all, she might've been afraid she'd forget my name. Sure, that's it! She must have wrote my name down that way so she'd remember it the next morning, figuring she'd thank me for driving her home the next time she saw me. That must be it. It's the only logical explanation, and it stands to reason. I'm an innocent man. I didn't kill her, and that's all I got to say.

I.O.: You don't expect us to believe all this crap, do you?

Suspect: That's my statement, Lieutenant. Type it up and I'll sign it.

I.O.: — — — —Strike that out, Steno!

Signed
        &   Billy T. Berkowitz
Typed   October 25, 1962

THE ALECTRYOMANCER

WHERE DID the old alectryomancer come from in the first place? I didn't see or hear him approach on the soft sand. I looked up from the sea and there he was, waiting patiently for me to recognize him. The blue denim rags covering his thin shanks were clean, and so was his faded blue work shirt. His dusky skin was the shade of wet number two emery paper, and he respectfully held a shredded brimmed straw hat in his right hand. Once he had my attention he nodded his head amiably and smiled, exposing toothless gums the color of a rotten mango.

"What do you want?" I said rudely. One of my chief reasons for renting a cottage on the tiny island of Bequia was the private beach.

"Please excuse my intrusion on your privacy, Mr. Waxman," the native said politely, "but when I heard that the author of *Cockfighting in the Zone of Interior* had rented a cottage on Princess Margaret Beach I wanted to congratulate him in person."

I was mollified, and at the same time, taken aback. Of course, I had written *Cockfighting in the Zone of Interior*, but it was a thin pamphlet, privately printed, issued in a limited edition of five hundred copies. The pamphlet had been written at the request of two well-heeled Florida cockfighters who had hoped to gain support for the sport from an eastern syndicate, and I had been paid more than the job was worth. But it certainly

Originally appeared in *Alfred Hitchcock's Mystery Magazine* as "A Genuine Alectryomancer," © 1959 by H.S.D. Publications, Inc.

wasn't the type of booklet to wind up in the hands of a Bequian native in the West Indies.

"Where did you get a copy of that?" I said, getting to my feet and brushing the damp sand off my swimming trunks.

"Gamecocks, Mr. Waxman, are my source of livelihood," he replied simply. "And I read everything I can find concerning gamefowl. Your pamphlet, sir, was highly informative."

"Thank you, but my information was excellent. I didn't know you fought gamecocks on Bequia, however. According to the British Mandate passed in 1857, cock-fighting was forbidden throughout the Empire."

"I don't fight gamecocks, Mr. Waxman." He smiled again and held up a protesting hand. "My interest in gamefowl lies in a parallel art: alectryomancy."

I laughed, but I was interested all the same. I had gone to Bequia because it was a peaceful little island in the Grenadines, and I had hoped to begin and finish a novel. But in three months time I hadn't written a line. Bored, and with little to do but stare sullenly at the sea, I found myself enjoying this curious encounter.

"That's a parallel art," I agreed good naturedly, "but I didn't know there were any practitioners of alectryomancy left in the Atomic Age."

"My rooster has made some fascinating predictions concerning the atom, Mr. Waxman," the alectryomancer confided. "If you would care to visit me sometime—at your convenience, of course—we could discuss his findings. Or possibly, you might be more interested in obtaining a personal reading—"

"I don't need any gamecock to make predictions for me," I said truthfully. "If I don't get some work done on my book soon I'll run out of money and be forced to return to the States and look for work."

"Isn't your writing going well?"

"It isn't going at all."

"Then there must be a reason. And only through alectryomancy can—"

I cut the interview short and returned to my cottage. After boiling some water for a cup of instant coffee and thinking about the odd meeting for a few minutes I concluded that there might be an article in the old man and his black art. Why not? Three or four thousand fast words on the old fellow's unusual occupation might conceivably find a market in the U.S., and I sure as hell wasn't getting anywhere with my novel project.

Alectryomancy, of course, is usually considered as a false science, on a par with astrology, if not as popular with the superstitious. A circle is described on the bare ground; the letters of the alphabet are then written around the outer edge of the circle and a grain or so of corn is placed on each letter. A rooster, preferably a cock from a gamestrain, is tethered to a stake in the center by his left leg, and then as he pecks a grain of corn from the various letters, the letters are written down by the alectryomancer, in order, and a message of—the "science" is crazy—really! For one thing, before there could be any validity to the message the rooster would have to be able to understand a language. And a chicken's brain is about the size of a BB. Still, an article about a practicing alectryomancer would be of interest to a great many readers, and I needed the money.

I didn't look the old alectryomancer up immediately; things are not done so speedily in the West Indies. I prepared myself for the impending interview by thinking about it for a couple of days, and then made my way to the seer's shack on Mount Pleasant. Bequia is a tiny island, and it was simple enough to find out where the old man lived.

"Where," I asked my simple-minded maid, "does the old man with the rooster live?"

It is to the woman's credit, I suppose, that she knew

to whom I referred, because every indigenous resident owns a few chickens and at least one rooster. She gave me directions I could understand, and even went so far as to draw a crude map with her finger on the sandy beach in front of the cottage.

Mount Pleasant is not a high mountain, as mountains go, but the path was crooked and steep and the forty-minute climb had winded me by the time I reached the old man's shack at the peak. He greeted me warmly and without surprise, and invited me to enjoy the lovely pano-rama of his view. Nine sea miles away the verdant, volcanic mass of St. Vincent loomed above the dark sea and, behind us toward the southwest, the smaller islands of the Grenadines glittered like emeralds in the sunlight.

"Your prospect is beautiful," I said, when I was breath-ing normally again.

"We like it, Mr. Waxman." The old native nodded his head.

"We?"

"My rooster and me."

"Oh, yes," I said casually, snapping my fingers. "I'd like to take a look at him."

At a low whistle from the alectryomancer the rooster marched sedately out of the shack and joined us in the clearing. He was a large whitish bird of about six or seven pounds, with brown and red feathers splashing his wings and chest. His limp comb was unclipped, and his dark red wattles dangled almost to his breast. He eyed me suspiciously for a moment, cocking his head alertly, and crowed deep in his throat as he stretched his long neck. He then turned away from us to scratch listlessly in the dirt.

"He looks like a Whitehackle cross," I observed.

"Correct, Mr. Waxman," the alectryomancer said re-spectfully. "His mother was a purebred *Gallus bankiva.*"

"I suspected as much. Only purebred gamecocks

should be utilized in alectryomancy, as you must know," I added pedantically.

"Of course."

For a few moments we sat quietly on the ground watching the stupid rooster, who was amusing himself by twisting his head sharply to the right, and then to the left, like a jay-walker looking for a lurking policeman. I cleared my throat. "As long as I'm here, I may as well have a reading."

"I'll change my clothes." The old man smiled, exposing his raw gums for my inspection, and then hobbled painfully into his shack.

The shack itself was reminiscent of the old Hooverville residences of the 1930's; it was built of five-gallon oil tins, smashed flat, and the roof was topped by a mauve fifty-gallon oil drum, which held, I presumed, rain water. Forming an even square around the clearing before the shack were several dozen five-gallon tins, each containing a young arrowroot plant. An alectryomancer, I supposed, wouldn't have too much business on a small island, and the arrowroot plants probably supplemented the old man's income.

I was unprepared for the change in attire and I started in spite of myself when the alectryomancer reappeared. A dirty white cotton turban had been wrapped around his bald head, and he wore a long-sleeved blue work shirt buttoned to the neck. Tiny red felt hearts, clubs, spades and diamonds had been sewn in thick profusion on the shirt, and larger card symbols had been sewn on the pair of faded khaki trousers he now wore instead of the ragged blue denim shorts. His splayed feet were still bare, however, which rather spoiled the effect.

"That's a unique costume, Mr.—?"

"Wainscoting. Two Moons Wainscoting. Thank you, sir."

"Is Two Moons your actual given name, Mr. Wainscoting?"

"You might say that. It was given to me when I was a small boy. My father took me across the channel in his fishing boat to St. Vincent when I was eleven years old. When I returned my friends asked me what I had seen over there. 'St. Vincent has a moon, too,' I told them. And I've been called Two Moons ever since."

"It's a romantic name, but quite appropriate for an alectryomancer."

"I have always regarded it highly. And now . . ." Two Moons tethered the Whitehackle cross to a stake in the clearing with a piece of brown twine, and proceeded to draw a circle around him with a pointed stick.

"The ancient Greeks," I said, to reveal to the man that I knew a few things about alectryomancy, "always described the circle on the ground *prior* to tethering the gamecock in the center."

"Yes," he agreed, and his face assumed for a moment a resentful expression, "but that isn't the way we do it in the West Indies. Every island race has its own traditions and rituals. I have nothing against the Greeks, and I can see some merit in describing the circle first, but on the other hand, it is possible that a portion of the circle will be rubbed out inadvertently when reentering the ring to tether the cock. I have tried both methods, and in all probability I shall use the Greek method again some time in the future. But the system employed doesn't affect the reading, or so I have learned through many years of experience."

"You could get into a technical argument on that statement."

"Undoubtedly. You can have an argument on any point pertaining to alectryomancy," Two Moons added cheerfully; and he began to draw the letters of the alphabet in a clockwise direction about the outer perimeter of the circle. He apparently took considerable pride in his work, drawing large block capital letters with his pointed stick, rubbing them out and doing them over gain when they didn't come up to his high standards. He measured the distances between each letter, using his stick as a ruler, and found it necessary to redraw the S and T because they were too close together.

"Now," he said when he was finished, surveying his handiwork, "the hard part is over. First, a personal question: what is your birth date, Mr. Waxman?"

"January 2, 1919."

"You'll have to speak a little louder, Mr. Waxman," Two Moons said apologetically. "My old rooster's beginning to get somewhat deaf, and I don't believe he heard you."

I repeated my birthday loudly, enunciating carefully for the rooster's benefit, although I felt rather foolish.

Two Moons paced counterclockwise about the circle, dropping a grain of corn in the center of each letter, and then sat beside me before signaling the bird with an abrupt motion of his pointed stick. The bird crowed, wheeled about twice, and pecked up the grain of corn on the letter M. Two Moons wrote M on the ground, and followed it with the O, R, and T as the chicken made his choices. After eating the fourth grain of corn, the rooster returned to the center of the circle, leaned wearily, almost dispiritedly, against the stake, and hung his head down to the ground. We waited, but it was quite evident from the apathy of the chicken that he was finished.

"Maybe he isn't hungry?" I suggested.

"We'll soon find out." Two Moons untied the cord from the rooster's left leg and carried him out of the circle. He scattered a few grains of corn, released the cock, and the bird scratched up and gobbled down cracked corn as if it were famished.

"He was hungry enough, Mr. Waxman; your reading is full and complete. M - O - R - T." Two Moons muttered the letters, savoring the sounds with his eyes half-closed.

"Mort. Tell me: is your middle name Mort, by any chance?"

"No. Harry Waxman, only. I dropped my middle name when I became a writer, but it wasn't Mort."

"Any relatives named Mort?"

I thought carefully. "No, none at all, not that I know of, anyway."

"That's too bad." Two Moons shook his head. "I had hoped . . ." His voice trailed away.

"Hoped what?"

"That Mort didn't mean what I knew in my heart that it did mean." He thumped his breast with a closed fist. "*Mort* is a French word meaning death, Mr. Waxman."

"So? How does it apply to me? I'm not a Frenchman; I'm an American. If the rooster's predicting anything about me he should do so in English. Right?"

"He doesn't know any English," Two Moons explained patiently. "I bought this rooster in Martinique, after my last gamecock died. All he knows is French. On difficult readings I often have to consult a French-English dictionary—"

"Maybe he was going to write 'MORTGAGE'?" I broke in.

"I sympathize with you, Mr. Waxman." Two Moons shook his head, almost dislodging his dirty turban. "But in alectryomancy we must go only by what the gamecock does write, not by what he does not. Otherwise—" He spread his hands wide, and shrugged hopelessly.

"Let's try another reading."

"Another time, perhaps. It's a nervous strain on my rooster, making predictions, and I only allow him to make one a day."

"Tomorrow, then," I said, getting to my feet.

"Perhaps tomorrow," he agreed reluctantly.

I took my wallet out of my hip pocket. "What do I owe you?"

"Nothing." The alectryomancer spread his arms, palms

up, and shrugged. "I would appreciate it, however, if you would be kind enough to autograph my copy of your pamphlet, *Cockfighting in the Zone of Interior*."

I felt my shirt pocket. "When I come up tomorrow. I didn't bring my fountain pen with me today—"

"If you don't mind, Mr. Waxman," Two Moons said reasonably. "In view of the prediction, I would prefer to have the autograph today. If you'll wait a moment, I have the pamphlet and a ballpoint pen inside the house . . ."

I slept fitfully that night, which meant little, if anything, to me. I had slept fitfully every night of the three months I had been on Bequia. No one had informed me of the fierceness of the sand flies on Princess Margaret Beach, and I had neglected to purchase a mosquito bar before departing from Trinidad. But between waking and sleeping, the prediction of the Whitehackle cross at least gave me something to think about. I was far from satisfied with Two Moons' interpretation of the word "mort."

The suggestion was too pat. And yet, as I lay there scratching in my bed, no better meaning suggested itself to me. Toward 2 A.M. I was reduced to considering M.O.R.T. as initials standing for a secret sentence of some kind. During the war I received several letters from a girl in California with S.W.A.K. written across the back of the envelope: this cryptic message meant "Sealed With A Kiss." But when this piece of romantic tripe crossed my mind I cursed myself as a fool, downed three searing tumblers of Mount Gay rum, and slept soundly until dawn.

By 8:30 A.M. I was on the mountain trail to Two Moons' metal residence. Halfway up the mountain I stopped for breath and a slow cigarette, regretting my decision to settle for coffee but no breakfast, and almost changed my mind about asking the old man for another reading. Curiosity and a few moments rest got the better of my judgment and I climbed on. When I topped the last crest to the clearing, Two Moons was seated cross-legged in the sunlight, humming happily, and plaiting a fish trap out of green palm leaf strips. He dropped his lower jaw the moment he saw me, and his yellow eye-balls popped in their sockets.

"Why, Mr. Waxman," he said, with well-feigned astonishment, "I didn't expect you this morning!"

"You needn't act so damned surprised," I scowled at him. "I told you I'd be back this morning."

"Please forgive my outburst; I apologize. But your case was remarkably similar to a reading I gave a student at Oxford, and I—"

"You attended Oxford?" It was my turn to be surprised.

"Baliol College, but for a year and a half only," Two Moons admitted modestly. "I was putting myself through college by practicing alectryomancy in London's West End. I had a poor but steady clientele; actors, actresses, producers, and two or three dozen playwrights."

"I fail to see how an Oxford man could end up back on Bequia," I said, looking at the Alectryomancer with new respect.

"An English Dom did it," Two Moons said ruefully.

"Got mixed up with a woman, eh?"

"No, sir. Not a woman, a Dom. A truly beautiful game-strain, the English Dom. Pure white, with a lemon bill and feet to match. I bought the rooster in Sussex, and before utilizing his services for my clients, I had him make a practice prediction for me. Without hesitating the Dom pecked out 'Bequia.' I ate the fowl as a farewell supper, packed my belongings, and departed on the next ship leaving England for Barbados. I've been here on Bequia ever since, thirty-two years this coming October."

"At any rate," I said, moved by the unhappy story, "one of your predictions came true."

"They all come true, when they are correctly interpreted by a skilled alectryomancer."

"We'll see. How about my second reading?"

"Yes, sir." Two Moons held out his right hand. "That will be ten dollars, please—in advance."

"Very well." I parted with a brown B.W.I. ten-dollar bill. "Bring on your French-pecking rooster."

The rigmarole was unchanged from the previous day. Two Moons changed from his blue denim shorts into his homemade costume and turban, tethered the gamecock, and drew the circle and block-letter alphabet as carefully as he had done for my first reading. He signaled with the pointed stick and the idiotic rooster pecked M, O, R, T and stopped. After crowing half-heartedly, the bird leaned against the stake with his head down, his bill touching the ground. I was unable to understand how the mere pecking up of four measly grains of corn could make the rooster so weary.

"Let's wait a bit, Two Moons." I cleared my dry throat. "Maybe he'll continue."

"As you wish, Mr. Waxman."

The minutes ticked away. The mid-morning sun was hot. The back of my neck stung with prickly heat. Mango flies and tiny eye gnats buzzed and feinted about my dripping face, but I waited. Five minutes, ten, fifteen minutes, and the rooster still remained immobilized in the center of the circle.

Two Moons clucked his tongue. "*Mort*," he said pityingly, "comes to us all, in time."

"An undeniable truth," I agreed indifferently, getting to my feet and stretching. "Well, thanks for the prediction, Two Moons. But it's a hot day and I'm going for a swim."

I started down the trail without a backward glance, my hands balled into tight fists inside the pockets of my khaki shorts.

"Watch out for barracuda," Two Moons shouted after me, "and the tricky cross currents!"

"Thanks!" I said drily, over my shoulder.

I didn't go swimming.

I didn't do anything.

I brooded. Sitting in the tiny living room of my screenless cottage, staring out the window at the bright blue, cheerful waters of the bay, I pondered dark thoughts. The first *mort* wasn't so bad, but when it came to two *morts* in a row I was forced to do a little quiet thinking. Like all Americans who consider themselves intelligent, I laugh at superstition. Ha ha! The pinch of salt, tossed carelessly over the shoulder—a meaningless precaution, but I did it all the time, without thinking about it. Did I ever place a hat upon a bed? Never! Why not? Well, just because, that's why. Did I ever walk under a ladder? No, of course not—a can of paint might spill over a man from above. That was prudence, not superstition. I wasn't really superstitious. Not really. It was just that that gamecock had been so positive, so cocksure. . . !

Three days later I fired my maid. The stubborn woman refused to taste my food, claiming falsely that she didn't like canned pork and beans. I issued an angry ultimatum, and when she still flatly but politely refused to eat a bite, and therefore prevent me from the possibility of being poisoned, I gave her the sack, and tossed the uneaten beans into the bay.

Without anyone else around the house, my life became more complicated, but I preferred to be alone. I had to meet the *M.V. Madinina* when she steamed into the harbor each Friday to get my provisions, and I had to have a list of foodstuffs ready to hand the captain. But I didn't mind the activity. I wasn't hungry, either, and the little I did eat was best prepared by myself. I woried, however. A bad tin of corned beef, a can of sour condensed milk, or even some undetected botulized canned string beans, and pouf! *Mort!* I drank a lot of Mount Gay rum, and very little water.

Three weeks after my second reading I paid a third visit to Two Moons Wainscoting. I was unable to stand the fear and suspense any longer; I needed additional, and concrete, information. I hadn't shaved for several days. Suppose I had cut myself with a rusty razor blade? Where could I get a tetanus shot on isolated Bequia? My sleep was no longer fitful; I couldn't sleep at all. Three full inches had disappeared from my waistline.

"Two Moons," I said anxiously, as soon as I stepped into his clearing, "I've got to have another reading."

"I've been expecting you, Mr. Waxman," Two Moons said sympathetically. "That is, I've been expecting word concerning you; but I must turn down your request for a third reading. This is not an arbitrary decision. The life of an alectryomancer on Bequia isn't an easy one, and I would welcome the prospect of another ten-dollar bill. But I am not a man totally lacking in compassion, so I must refuse—"

"I'll give you twenty dollars—"

Two Moons held up a hand to silence me. "Please, Mr. Waxman. My decision is not a matter of mere money! Let me summarize: you have had two flat predictions, both of them identical. *Mort!* An ugly word, whether in English or French, but *mort* all the same. Suppose, on a third prediction, that my gamecock were to peck out a W.E.D.S., or even a simple F.R.I.? Do you see the implications? You're a writer, Mr. Waxman; you are not without imagination. A gamecock is incapable of deceit, of deliberately telling a falsehood; and if my rooster pecked F.R.I.—which he could do in all innocence—this is the abbreviation for 'Friday.' Today is Tuesday. How would you feel tomorrow, on Wednesday? And then Thursday? The next day would be Friday, and Friday would be the day for what? *Mort!*" He pointed a long brown forefinger at my chest, and shook his head unhappily.

A shudder danced icily down my spine. "But—"

"Please, Mr. Waxman. I simply cannot risk another reading. An alectryomancer has a conscience, just like everyone else, and I would suffer along with you, so I must refuse your request for a third reading. I cannot; I will not do it!"

"I'm a young man," I croaked hoarsely, "and I'm not ready to die. I'm barely into my forties—the prime of life."

"Well," Two Moons pursed his lips, "there's an alternative." He peered at me intently. "But I hesitate to mention it to a man with so little faith."

"Mention it," I said sharply. "By all means, mention it."

"Are you cognizant of the West Indian *obeah*?"

"I think so. It's a spell or charm of some kind, isn't it?"

"In a way, yes. There are all kinds of *obeah*; they can be made for good or evil, just as African *ju-jus* are made for good or evil. Unfortunately," he sighed, "many West Indians have a vindictive character, and they often cast about for a means of vengeance for a very small grievance. This deplorable trait of character, I am happy to state, is not a universal West Indian—"

"Right now," I broke in, "I'm not interested in the character traits of the average West Indian. I have problems of my own."

"To be sure. To shorten the rather interesting story I was preparing to tell you, I possess an *obeah* that will ward off *mort* for an indefinite period."

"Let me take a look at it."

"Not so fast. Like all spells, charms, and *ju-jus*, an *obeah* also has a condition attached."

"What are the conditions?"

"Condition." He raised a long forefinger. "Singular, Mr. Waxman. A simple condition, but a condition nevertheless. Belief. Blind, unquestioning belief. So long as you believe in the *obeah* you shall have life. Not everlasting life, as is promised by your optimistic Christian *obeahs*, but life for a reasonable period of time. The Grenadian who fashioned this *obeah*, for example, lived to be one hundred and ten."

"That's a long time."

"A very long time."

"I believe," I said quickly. "Give me the *obeah!*"

"You are an impulsive young man, Mr. Waxman. This is a valuable *obeah*, and before I can consider giving it to you I must test your belief. The *obeah* has a price of seventy-five dollars."

I passed the test.

Happier than I had been in days I ran down the mountain trail, a small leather sack tied around my neck. The sack was securely fastened with a square knot in the rawhide thong at the back of my neck, and from time to time I fingered the knot to make certain it wouldn't slip.

Night fell. I sat in my tiny living room, trying to relax with a cigar and a light grog. The pale light of my kerosene lamp—there is no electricity on Bequia—made my shadow dance on the wall like a boxer. The wind, as well as my quick, inadvertent movements, was responsible for my flickering shadow, but I felt like a boxer, fighting the deadly logic of the gamecock's prediction. I clutched the thick leather sack at my neck, feeling vaguely the strange objects inside, wondering what in the devil they were. Two Moons had warned me not to look inside— "Never look a gift horse in the mouth"—were his exact words, but I was curious all the same. If I stopped believing in the *obeah*, death—*mort*—could strike me suddenly, at any moment. The great wisdom of Two Moons Wainscoting, in denying me a third, and final, prediction, was the only bright spot in my thinking. Even with the *obeah* in my possession, I couldn't live forever . . .

Not that I had any particular reason to go on living, to extend my life for an indefinite period. I wasn't happy now, and I never had been happy. I was single, no dependents, no real purpose in life—really, except for the writing of novels, and an occasional short story. But I wanted to hang on, if for no other reason than to see what would happen next. I had lost all désire to write an article on alectryomancy.

I fingered the strange objects inside the *obeah* sack. What were they? Why did they have this mysterious power? I jerked my hand away quickly. What if my fingers recognized one or more of the objects inside the leather sack? How could I go on believing in the efficacy of the *obeah*, if I discovered what the sack contained? A nasty situation, all the way around.

In the daytime, life wasn't so bad. The bright sunlight and blue skies chased away the problems of the night. But everything I did, which wasn't much, was done judiciously, carefully. I still swam every day, but never ventured more than a few yards from shore, fearing the treacherous cross currents. I continued to take daily hikes, but I walked slowly, like an old man with brittle bones. And I carried a cane. Most of the time I sat quietly on the narrow front porch of my cottage drinking rum and water, staring moodily at the sea. The *obeah* was doing a good job of protecting me from accidental death, but sometimes I wished that *mort* would come to me in the night, in my sleep, so that it would be all over and done with.

After a few lonely, disconsolate evenings I began to go to the hotel in the evenings, picking my way along the beach path, playing my flashlight on every shadow before taking another cautious step. There wasn't any electricity at the hotel either, but the verandah and small outside bar were lighted by Coleman lanterns, and they didn't cast shadows.

Just a few short hours ago I was sitting at a wicker table on the hotel verandah staring glumly into my glass, when Bob Corbett sat down across from me. One quick glance at his red, serious face and orange moustache, and I shook my head.

"No. No nattering tonight, Bob," I said firmly. "I'm not up to it."

Bob Corbett had one of those vague British civil service jobs that seemed to provide him with more free time than work. He made periodic trips to various islands looking for fungus or something, but the government provided a house for him on Bequia—although he did not have an office. Like many of the bored civil servants posted to the Windward Islands for three years, Bob had become addicted to the game of "nattering." Nattering is a kind of game where two persons trade insults until one of them gets angry enough to fight. The person who has the best self-control wins, even though he ends up more often than not with a bloody nose. During the apprentice years of my writing career I had served time as a desk clerk at a Los Angeles hotel for almost two years and, as a consequence, I had bested Bob Corbett in every nattering session he started. In the last set-to we played, Bob had taken a swing at me with an empty Black & White bottle.

"No nattering," Bob agreed readily, signaling the barmaid to refill our glasses. "I came over to make amends, to tell you the truth. I've been standing at the bar for almost an hour without a sign of recognition from you, and if it's an apology you want you can have it. But I really didn't hit you with that bottle, old man—"

"I'm sorry, Bob. I didn't cut you on purpose; I didn't see you," I apologized. All at once, I felt an overwhelming desire to confide in Bob Corbett, to take advantage of his unimaginative common sense, and I yielded impulsively to the desire. The dark thoughts had been bottled up inside me too long; I had to get them out into the open.

"Listen, Bob," I began, "did you ever hear of alectryomancy?" And I unfolded the whole story, from my first meeting with Two Moons on the beach.

"Ho-ho-ho!" Bob laughed wetly, when I had finished. "You've been had, old man!"

"What're you talking about?"

"Had. Taken. Bilked! And you're a Californian, too! That's what makes it so funny!" Another string of bubbling ho-ho-hos followed, and I drummed my fingers impatiently on the table.

"Old Two Moons is a notorious character in the islands, Harry," Bob said at last, wiping the corners of his eyes with the back of his freckled left hand. "This old faker and his trained rooster have caused I don't know how many complaints to the Administrator on St. Vincent from irate tourists. His rooster, you see, is trained to peck out the word '*mort*'! And the convincing mumbo-jumbo Two Moons puts with it has sucked you in. That's all."

"I don't believe you, Bob. I'd like to, but I can't."

"I'll prove it to you," Bob said, leaning across the table. "After the rooster pecked the four grains of corn, ostensibly spelling '*mort*,' he hung his head down. Right?"

"Right."

"Following this, then, didn't Two Moons remove the chicken from the circle and feed him some more corn? And didn't the rooster scratch it up and eat it?"

"Of course. That's what made the reading so effective."

"No, Harry. It proves only that the rooster is trained. Think a bit, man. To train animals of any kind, you must always reward them with food after they do their trick. And food is the only reward an animal recognizes! A trained rooster is no different from a trained bear that's been given a bottle of beer for doing a dance. A bloke I knew in Newfoundland had a bloody wolf chained in his garage, and one—"

I left the table, not waiting to hear about the bloody wolf in Newfoundland, and, flashing my torch before me, ran all the way home along the beach path. As soon as my kerosene lamp was lighted, and the wick trimmed, I untied the thong at the back of my neck, and dumped the contents of the leather sack on the dining table. Inventory: one plastic toothpick (red); one round, highly polished obsidian pebble; two withered jackfish eyes (lacquered); one dried chameleon tail, approximately three inches long; one red chess pawn (plastic); three battered and curiously bent Coca-Cola bottle caps; one chicken feather (yellow); six assorted and unidentifiable (to me) small dried bones; and one brass disc entitling the bearer to a ten-cent beer at Freddy Ming's Cafe, Port-of-Spain, Trinidad.

A scorching red film seared my eyes. I stared stupidly at the contents of the *obeah* and cursed Two Moons Wainscoting aloud for at least five minutes. Then I scooped the objects into the leather sack, tightened the thong drawstring, went outside, and tossed the thing into the sea. The buoyant sack floated on the surface, bobbing gently, drifting away from the shore on the outgoing tide. Still sullen with anger, a great idea occurred to me. I would recover the *obeah* from the sea, pay a return visit to Two Moons' establishment—and feed him each object in the bag, one at a time.

This idea delighted me so much I kicked off my sandals, on impulse, waded into the water, and then dived after the *obeah*, which was now sailing away from me as though it were fitted out with a spinnaker. I soon found, with mounting apprehension, that in spite of all the strokes I was taking, I wasn't making much headway. The *obeah* floated, bobbing, just beyond my grasp, while the riptide tore at my chest and shorts. I panicked, and as my strokes grew weaker I knew that the *obeah* was my only hope of salvation; and yet it always floated, tantalizing me, just beyond my grasp. The night was so black I didn't even know where the land was anymore, and I began to think about the night-feeding barracuda—

"*Obeah!*" I screamed. "*I believe in you! I believe, I*

believe, I believe! I—" An angry wave crashed against my open mouth.

When I regained consciousness, dawn was showing itself whitely in the sea pools along the shore, although the sky was still as dark as polaroid glass. I was waterlogged and, for longer than I care to remember, I was sick to my stomach. Despite my weakness and nausea, however, I was filled with a wild, almost overwhelming sense of elation: the *obeah* was clutched tightly in my right hand!

At last I staggered to my feet, and, bent almost double by my cramping stomach, I made my way weakly down the beach toward my cottage. I had the title—*This Is My God*—and most of the first chapter of my novel outlined in my mind, and I was anxious to get these words on paper while the details were fresh and pure.

THE END